ANTHOLOGY
OF APPARITIONS

SIMON LIBERATI

ANTHOLOGY
OF
APPARITIONS

PUSHKIN PRESS
LONDON

With thanks to the barmen at
Le Select, Café de Flore, Ferde, La Palette
and the café of the Jardins de Luxembourg

Original text © Flammarion
Anthology of Apparitions first published in French
as *Anthologie des apparitions* in 2004

Translation copyright
© Paul Buck, Catherine Petit & Pushkin Press 2005
Special thanks to Christopher Scott Vann

This edition first published in 2005 by
Pushkin Press
12 Chester Terrace
London NW1 4ND

British Library Cataloguing in Publication Data:
A catalogue record for this book is available
from the British Library

ISBN 1 901 285 58 8

Cover: *Untitled*
© Thomas Nützl
Frontispiece: Author photograph
© Nicolas Hidrioglou

Set in 10 on 12 Monotype Baskerville
and printed in Britain
by Blacketts, Epping, Essex

ANTHOLOGY
OF APPARITIONS

CLAUDE WAS SITTING at the Zodiaque, a café at the Porte des Lilas in Paris, reading *Introduction to the Devout Life* by St Francis de Sales, when he saw little Veronique, looking the same as ever. Twenty-five years later and she hadn't aged, it even seemed that she was still wearing her cobra-skin patent stilettos from Messageries with her old rabbit fur wrapped around her arm. "This area is dodgy," she said to him. "I heard your sister is dead." Claude couldn't answer her because his mobile was ringing. It was Ali: "Just to say I met an Israeli producer of action films. He works with people like Steven Seagal and Jean-Claude Van Damme. He might be small in size, but he has a big spirit … "

Claude thanked him, but explained that he didn't see why he bothered to call just to tell him that. When he looked up Veronique was no longer there.

Claude's sister, Marina, had disappeared years ago. He still had the last postcard she sent him, dated the 1st March 1985. It showed Jayne Mansfield and her children with lions. On the card was written: "Everything's fine. How are you? Your little pagan idol embraces you, Marina." Claude knew his sister was seeing the same type of people in Los Angeles as she had in Paris, namely Victoria S, the daughter of a famous comic actor, who was later implicated in the Heidi Fleiss prostitution scandal. Marina disappeared one evening in June 1987 and nobody had heard from her since.

She was christened Annie, but as soon as she reached adulthood, around twelve years old, she took another, as did many of their friends back then. Everybody in the set called her 'little Marina'. At the time, the newcomers, often very young, were designated by their first name (or their pseudonym) preceded by the epithet 'little'. Thus: 'little Christophe', 'little

Justine', 'little Marceline', 'little Pierre', 'little Vincent', 'little Fred', 'little Veronique' and 'little Marina'.

Little Marina was Claude's younger sister, but his elder in every way. While Claude was still at school, she went out with adults who initiated her very early into the world of cruel human truths. She was the one who taught her brother, for example, never to get into a car with diplomatic number plates, or to avoid hanging around with people she judged as 'dodgy'. In such matters her judgment was quite sane.

Between 1978 and 1980 they lived together in Paris in a studio near rue Saint-Denis. Their days began around three in the afternoon and rarely finished before eight in the morning. They nourished themselves with hot dogs from the takeaway downstairs, and gin & tonic with blue curacao. Marina consecrated a large part of her day to making herself beautiful. Girls from her set would come round and they talked as they did each others' hair and nails. Claude stayed in bed reading old copies of *Paris-Match*, or *Marie-Claire*, or even, for a laugh, the jobs section in *Le Figaro*.

"Pauline, what's a telex operator?"

"Umm, I think it's someone who sends telexes."

"What's a telex?"

"I don't know, leave me the fuck alone."

Often one of Marina's friends would join him in bed and together they would look at photos of actresses.

"Wow! Anita Ekberg's cobra-skin stilettos, I want some of those. Did you see them, Marina?"

When she leaned across to show the photo, Claude felt Pauline or crazy Veronique's body against his, but it didn't excite him. It was just warmth, like some kind of affection between animals of the same breed and of the same litter. They would possibly have sex later on, or rather they would 'give their bodies' as they used to say. It would be by chance, and even for free, but not before four in the morning. In their set, one wasn't sensual, one didn't enjoy sex. Hippie things like pleasure or sexual freedom, they didn't give a shit about that. Their thing was parading around with beautiful hair and the right kit. If some old john wanted to get off, that was his problem. They didn't even always ask for money, what did they know, or really care, as long as the sucker had 'classy wheels' or a 'nice place' (preferably in the vicinity) and one could 'work' his telephone or take other advantages in kind.

"Eva's going out with a new guy: he's called Kung Fu. He has a classy American car with calf-skin seats."

"Leather?"

"No. I said: calf-skin."

The precisely painted mouth from which issued these childish words was that of 'crazy Veronique'. Skinny and cold as a junkie even before she was one, she had an 'icy blonde' style copied from the actress Eva-Marie Saint, whom she resembled a bit. She was painting Marina's toenails and Claude could see her bird-like profile. I don't know if Eva Marie Saint wore her hair in a bee-hive but Veronique's was absolutely phenomenal. A good twenty centimetres high, as smooth as an ostrich egg, it must have cost her a bomb in lacquer every day. Veronique worked as an usherette at the Théâtre des Innocents, an erotic theatre on the Place des Innocents. Nobody ever talked about it, eroticism was even less her thing than it was for the others. On the other hand she loved to gossip about her girlfriends' pick ups.

"They say that F works at Madame Claude's."

"Who told you that?"

"ABS. His sister told him."

"How much do you think she makes for a fuck?"

"He told me eight thousand."

"Uh—That's bollocks."

"Yeah, but it's a whole night with an emir."

"So what, it's not because he's an Arab that he's an idiot."

Marina knew what she was talking about. One summer she had lived in Cannes with some guys from the Persian Gulf. It was '76, she was fourteen, and Zaza, the friend she was with, was thirteen. Even if she didn't let on to Veronique.

"Bitch, look, you just fucked up my toenails."

"Eh, you don't talk to me like that."

Around seven in the evening the girls went out visiting.

"Come on, we're going to Kruger's."

"I'm sure he's put a padlock on his fridge and another on the phone."

Sometimes Marina went out alone, all ornamented and brocaded like a courtesan from Petronius. For nothing. To phone from a booth. Sometimes just to go down to the Felix Potin grocery on the corner. Claude often stayed by himself, through laziness or melancholy, or simply because he was not a girl. Through the window he could hear the sewing machines of the neighbouring workshops and he could see sunlight on the cracks of the facing wall. He wrote short poems (never longer than two lines) like:

Did you lose your Giton, Pannychis
Your Giton, the colour of gingerbread grease?

The voice-mail on Claude's mobile rang. It was Ali: "I'm phoning to know if Elisabeth R is a swinger." The rest of the message was inaudible. Ali had read somewhere that Marcel Proust kept note cards on his contemporaries. Since then his card index was worthy of the Gestapo.

"If I don't write my book, at least I can unload them on the police."

Jokingly, Claude often told his comrade that no service would be interested in cards basically fifteen years out of date. Nevertheless he showed Marina's letters to Ali to see if he knew the people mentioned in them.

"Aha, Victoria S! Look, I have an old *American Playboy* from '86 with photos of her."

Claude stopped him when it became obvious that he knew nothing about Victoria S. On the other hand Marina's last postcard inspired Ali, especially the picture on the back. Claude pointed out the hairdo, characteristic of the movie star in her declining years.

"You see, Jayne Mansfield, she's wearing her last wig … The same hairpiece that got stuck in the windscreen when her head smashed."

"Hey, look! She's wearing the same boots as the day she died."

Ali had taken from an Italian book a police shot taken in New Orleans on the night of the accident. In the foreground, under a blanket, Jayne Mansfield's body, with her boots half undone. Views of dead people in photos interested them both.

"Maybe she was poor, right," Ali resumed, "but a star just doesn't keep the same pair of shoes for more than six weeks. It's a matter of image. The picture on the postcard must date from the beginning of '67. Those children are hers, they're already grown-up. She must've been decapitated a few weeks later. Do you know who this is in the photo with Jayne? That bearded guy, there … "

"No."

"That's Anton La Vey, the guy who founded the Church of Satan, a loony guru-type. The lions are his. I wonder where your sister could've bought such a postcard. Do you think Jayne … I mean, Marina, attended Black Masses?"

Claude remained silent. He and Ali had a common interest in details: dates, wigs, shoes, in the vague hope that the essential—work, love, death … real death, not movie star death—would elude them completely. But sometimes they would come across essentials by chance. The end of Jayne Mansfield's life had been marked by Satanism, and Claude had the impression that his sister's had as well.

Suddenly Ali's attention was caught by another of Marina's letters, the one just before, dated '84, written on torn headed notepaper that ended with:

"I embrace you and Niki too."

"Niki, that's the name of a whore. I knew a Niki at Madame Claude's who used to sleep with one of Polanski's pals. A Eurasian, I think she left for the States. Wait, I must have her card."

While Ali was looking for her card, Claude looked through the window at Paris, the dirty chestnut trees, the pigeons, the Arabs, the church on the square below, ugly but benevolent.

Niki (real name and surname unknown). Undoubtedly N, met on 12.5.78 at the Élysée-Matignon. Told me she 'works in movies'. Bullshit, of course. Slept with her. She bragged about giving blowjob to Alain Delon. To flatter me says that Alain and I have the same dick. Lives in a studio Boulevard Lannes. No name on the door. In the morning someone called 'Yasmine' phones. Perhaps Yasmine S?

"Who's Yasmine S?"

"When Madame Claude fell, her network continued to function for a while. The empire was managed by two sisters: Yasmine and Christelle S. I also know that they—both of them—slept with their step-father. At least one has since died of Aids. To be confirmed."

"Have you finished the card?"

Seen again on the 4.9.78, still at the Élysée-Matignon, pretends not to see me because she's sitting at Klaus Kinski's table with another drugged up Eurasian girl.

Seen again on the 30.11.79 at Club 78. (Evening when Baron Empain slapped Elli Medeiros across the face.) She is with a friend of Polanski, who works with the producer Claude Berri. This time she talks to me, says she's leaving for the States, because Britt Ekland's agent has her under contract. Sounds bullshit to me. I think she's a whore.

23.5.82. Heard talk of her via Lindo, ex-bouncer at the Bain Douche, met at the Apocalypse. He confirms that she is a whore and left for Los Angeles last year to set up a hairdressing salon with a girlfriend. To check because Lindo is not always very reliable.

"That's it, it stops there. See, my card is all yellowish."

Ali beamed. The large eyes of this ex-beau, now fallen on hard times, were rolling at the reminiscence of his busy youth.

"You do remember! At the time we were doing wonderful boys and girls and we didn't give a shit."

"They probably felt the same."

To quiet him, Claude recited those appropriate lines from I don't know which French poet of the eighteenth century:
We knew how to make the most of time
When you gave yourself for free.

But Ali wasn't listening. He asked Claude, "Is my hair okay, or what?" while taking a family-size hair spray from a shaggy shoulder-bag.

"She is OK, auntie," (auntie was him) "she has aged well, don't you think?"

" … "

"Anyway, it's true that officially, I'm only thirty-eight. Someone told me the other day that I looked much younger than my age. Do you know that Claude Montana never stops eyeing me? He's crazy about Arabs."

Claude looked at Ali's shiny nose on which blackheads had erupted into slagheaps and his hair-implants lined up like rows of leeks. He looked at least fifty, which of course was not a lot compared to the Apollo Belvedere, but too much for a not well-off bisexual living in a two-room bed-sit thirty-seven metres square. Claude reminded him that between them they had more than ninety years. Ali became philosophical.

"We're lucky to still be alive. When I think about the cemetery around us."

And he listed once more the necrology of their deceased friends: Marina, Sophie K, Little Laure, Jean-Marc F, Eric P, Laure T, Philippe S and Francisco U.

"Stop, it sounds like the visitor's book at Roblot's funeral parlour."

Ali went to the loo. Claude leafed through a copy of *Vanity Fair* lying near his friend's box of spliffs. A photo of Elisabeth Saltzmann with Medora Du Bonnet; nice shoes. Ali's voice came from the cubicle as if from a confessional.

"Tell me the truth, did you have it off with Marina?"

"Of course, everyone sleeps with their sister. Especially mine. Show me more cards, in the end they're really funny."

"Yeah, I'm going to use them to write my book. I've already thought up a title."

"Let me guess. I've got it … *The Losers*."

"No. *Anthology of Apparitions*."

"That's nice."

An old tatty card had fallen on the floor. Claude leaned forward to pick it up and asked Ali, through the loo door:

"Tell me, who is this Romina Power."

"Romina Power's the daughter of Tyrone Power, the famous American actor. She was a singer in Italy."

"Did you fuck?"

"Tyrone?"

"No, his daughter."

"No, but I drank from her glass in Rome, at the Jackie O in '76."

"Is she dead too?"

"No, I don't think so."

"Cool!"

CLAUDE, IN SPITE OF PRETENDING he didn't care, was sad to be a loser. Not that he wanted to own the things he could not afford, like a plasma-screen television, a Mercedes convertible and other gadgets, but he would have liked to have some peace after all these years. A beautiful nineteenth century house in the countryside, a garden. Instead of which he was queuing up at social security in the nineteenth district every three months for the renewal of his income support.

First queue at reception, then take a number and wait. Two hours on average. As he didn't really feel like a tramp, wasting his time didn't upset him. He had noticed, in fact, that the tramps were always the most hurried, trying to overtake the Arabs as if they had something to do, as if someone was waiting for them. Often they left, having lost patience, without seeing the social workers. As for the Arabs, that was altogether another story. They never had the right papers, they didn't understand what was explained to them, and they ended up by getting annoyed. As for the blacks, or at least, the black women—the men never turned up—they specialized in screaming kids smelling of poo.

Everybody has limits, for him it was the children. Although he found little piccaninnies charming compared to French ones, screaming was never agreeable. Generally, Claude took his number and went to the bar opposite to read, for example, the *Introduction to the Devout Life* or *The Life of Rancé*. The only thing that saved him in all the waiting (when one is poor, one waits a lot) was reading.

Marina had taken this paperback, *The Life of Rancé* by Chateaubriand, to that notorious picnic in the countryside on the banks of the Senlis canal. She never managed to open it because they had remained lying on the grass, watching the big white clouds of the Île-de-France pass across the sky.

15

There was Noc, an ex-Miss Thailand, Niki, and Kim—later called Lychee—and also a Chinese guy they called David-Alexandre Winter because of his out-dated haircut. All lost people, slightly dazed by the daylight. People who had nothing to do with the beautiful French countryside, the hedges of hornbeams and blackthorns, the big fat white clouds and the washed light of June. People as misplaced in this landscape as stained velvet benches on the pavement in the middle of the day when a nightclub is being renovated. All these beautiful people had piled into two cars one morning after leaving the Babylone, and had decided to go and have a picnic. On the menu, Laotian sausages and rice alcohol. The transvestites were jabbering in Thai. Marina leaned her head on Claude.

"If I had a child, what would we call it?"

"Medora, like the daughter of Lord Byron and his sister."

"They had a child too?"

"Stop saying *too*. We'll never have a child."

"Why? I'm old enough."

"It would be a monster."

"What did you say? Fedora?"

"Medora, with a M, like Mary Poppins."

"Sounds like a dog's name. I saw a clairvoyant you know, and she told me I was going on a long journey."

"Perhaps you're going to die and she didn't dare tell you."

"Death, I love it. Will you come and get me out of hell?"

At that moment, a creature in the grass bit Marina, who went wild, certain that it was a viper. With that, she no longer adored death, and she found them all hopeless at providing medicine, first aid, comfort, and the last sacrament. The child and the long journey; all was forgotten. She became very angry. It was the anger of a heroin addict, the anger of a mad woman against everything and everyone, Claude, the transvestites, even poor David-Alexandre Winter who took an interest in her misfortune with the compassion of a gay nurse. She left them there. She hitchhiked and returned to Paris in a van—apparently. Claude was used to it, so he stayed, lying on the ground, watching the big clouds pass across the royal-blue sky and, he remembered, he fell asleep.

It was the same impassive clouds, like dead sperm whales, that he saw reflected in the windows of the social security office some twenty years later. Chateaubriand was a childhood memory, from when their father made them learn entire passages of *The Life of Rancé* by heart. Marina he forced especially—Annie, at the time—because he smelt that her youth was going out of control. He wanted to give his daughter a sense of taste, something that would protect her from mediocrity. Thus, like a mynah bird, at the age of ten she would shout in the bus:

Societies long since vanished, how many have succeeded you! Dances founded on the dust of the dead, and tombs growing beneath steps of joy. We laugh and sing in the places soaked in the blood of our friends. Where today are yesterday's sorrows? What importance should we attach to worldly things?

Claude remembered that later, at the Élysée-Matignon, she had recited this passage to a guy who introduced himself as the 'majority director' of a NewMan boutique and who proposed that they 'help themselves to his bottle'. When he heard the little one reciting Chateaubriand, the man went completely wild. "Can you entrust me with your girlfriend for the night?" he said to Claude. "It's not with my dick that I love her, it's with my soul. It's psychic." The next day, Marina told Claude the man had offered her five hundred francs to piss in his mouth.

Deep down, Claude had always preferred idleness to work. Thus, to go and ask every three months for his social security from the rather kindly-disposed social workers, definitely kinder than an employee of a temp-agency or someone in personnel, didn't humiliate him in the slightest. It's in good taste to be moved by poverty. But Claude found poverty rather agreeable.

It was like being well-off, but quieter. You didn't have to do anything, you had time to shop. Except you don't have the money. So you do a slightly more pitiful shopping than other people, but not so bad with the stuff you buy from tramps, or Arab shops (like Guerifrippes or Bébertsoldes), or at Ed, the discount-grocery chain, or in the ten-franc shops. For those interested, you can enjoy sexual pleasure up to a point, more than people who have to work. Otherwise one waits, all the time, in queues, for phone calls, problems, friends, a partner's footsteps on the stairs, sleep and, of course, death. Attention, Claude didn't prostitute himself at the rue Marx-Dormoy social security office for peanuts. He received more than the average: social security for a couple amounted to 3,828 francs a month at the time. As always, he 'fooled' them a bit. N (called Niki), his wife, had left ten years earlier, but they didn't have to know that. He was still laughing, thinking about Ali who had taken out Niki's card. Those cards really weren't up-to-date. Ali had never known they were married. Closing the book, Claude thought once again that Rancé had good reason to leave for the convent. When love is dead, when the decapitated head of your lover is placed on your night-table, when everything is consumed, how good it must be to withdraw to the countryside after a beautiful wasted youth. But for that one needs money ... and to have seen your mistress's head decapitated. Alas, Claude had nothing to repent. Marina had vanished into thin air and N had taken refuge in Belgium, with an old antique dealer.

Coming out of the bar and going back to the Wailing Wall of the nineteenth district, he saw his reflection in a shop window: boots two sizes too big with elasticated sides as slack as an old pair of underpants, a greenish pair of jeans, a fake Oxford shirt from Guerifrippes, and hair plastered down like *papier-mâché* with yellow hair cream bought for six francs from the blacks at the Palais Rochechouart. At such moments one has to love oneself a lot. But, boys are much cleverer at loving themselves then girls. Ultimately, one holds the gaze of the others, for when one has been handsome, one is handsome forever. And Claude was right: an old fag, a kind of male Golda Meir or female Arafat, was leering at him.

With him, the female social workers were 'a walkover'—as Niki would have said. They were already so pleased to see a Frenchman from France, who had neatly filled in their forms, was polite with the ladies and understood what they said to him. One day, on top of it, he was getting help from a long-necked blonde. Rare, a long neck on a social worker. When she turned her head towards her files, she even looked, ever so slightly, and through squinted eyes, like Natalie Paley—yes, educated gay reader, you've read it right. Her hands however, left a lot to be desired. Stubby, somewhat reddish, bad circulation. Claude could predict without too many mistakes that they were acquainted with washing up liquid, toilet cleaner and the office manager's balls. He looked at her shoes, square-heeled casuals from André or Bata with blue leather uppers and straps, worn with thick tights to conceal her farmyard calves. But the upper body, from the sloping shoulders to the blond wave: Natalie Paley.

While she was asking him the usual questions about the hypothetical insertion which justified his minimum income, he saw again the image of Natalie Paley with a certain Mary Taylor, that Marina had taped above their mattress in the rue du Caire.

In the middle of the picture was an enormous shadow of a candelabra, projected as in a Chinese shadow-theatre, suspended far too low in an oppressive vampire-like way, above the plaster bust of a neo-classic Apollo, Mapplethorpe-style, curiously decorated with a black tulle ribbon. Two women were seated, as in a theatre and lit by a spotlight. Their gazes were symmetrically carried outward towards the edges of the photo. Their busts slightly turned away and their heads firmly opposed. They didn't look at each other. The angelic body of the one on the left was tightly clad in a long light coloured silk dress with small buttons. One of her arms was hanging, abandoned in the position of a dying swan; the other arm

19

was propped on a pedestal—cut by the framing—topped by a second sculpture, and was folded, the back of her open hand resting on her cheekbone, not far from a deep-set melancholic shadowed eye and overexposed white flesh. This one was the Russian, the niece of the last Tsar, Natalie Paley.

"Do you know that you can have one electricity bill per winter reimbursed by going to the social services in the eighteenth district, rue Ordener?"

Claude did not dare to tell the pseudo-Natalie Paley that the electricity company had cut off his supply and that he was us-ing candles to light his studio-apartment and that he liked that better for he found the light more dramatic. Instead, he nod-ded with the weak and panic-stricken air he was always taking when practical people wanted to help him.

"Do you understand what I'm telling you? Do you want me to write it all down?"

The tone of the social worker clearly showed what she thought of people like him. To protect himself from this new intrusive reality which didn't concern him, he called for the help of the real Natalie Paley and above all Mimsy Taylor, the second woman in the picture.

Mary Taylor, called 'Mimsy' Taylor: an American teenager who looked so much like Marina that one would have thought she was a reincarnation. The fifteen-year-old was posing in the picture because she was going to die. At least that was what the doctors told her parents. One year to live. Subsequently, her parents offered her anything she wanted: a tour of the world, beautiful dresses, permission to stay out till seven in the morn-ing. Every girl's dream. Some would catch fatal diseases for less. Or invent them. Perhaps it was her case: dressed all in black, the condemned nymphet had nice chubby cheeks for one about to die. Not the least sign of chlorosis. Marina used to say that they shared the same air of a 'piglet with strong jaws'. And it was not the only thing they shared: Marina had also been condemned by medicine when she was twelve. Emancipation followed: Le 7 in rue Sainte-Anne, the clubs, the movie-star life, while Claude continued with school. But, of course, the little one was soon dragging her brother along. Both wanted to live as in the twenties or in the Italian metaphysical films of the sixties: Antonioni, Fellini and company. But as they didn't have the means, the *dolce vita*, all the *notte* they had known, happened through dodging, muddling, or simply the generosity of their intimate friends. Sixteen years old, fresh as roses, they already felt like losers, wading through the flea market at Montreuil on Monday mornings, already hanging out with niggers, already scrimping over a jacket worth five francs. The Festival at Cannes, the grand hotels in Cabourg, all that happened through borrowing an old queen's car, stealing somebody else's invitation or drinking from Romina Power's glass.

Finally, Claude's social worker let him go.

Golda Meir was waiting for him outside. Surely there was two hundred francs in it if he agreed to give a quick blow job. Passing in front of the café, he heard Radio Nostalgie: *Il faut beau il fait chaud le printemps court dans les ruisseaux ...* He tried to find some beauty in the man—everybody's got something. In this man's case there was nothing. Or maybe something Claude didn't want to see. He let it drop, for, as Niki used to say: 'When you're a hundred per cent disgusted, don't go there'.

IT SHOULD BE SAID right away: Claude never seriously tried to find out what happened to his sister. That effort was beyond his capabilities. At the beginning, his wife N called Niki was enough to replace her. Until the day he lost her too, in a tourist-trap nightclub in Palma de Mallorca.

There are cheap hotels with names like 'Marina del sol' in Palma on the Paseo Maritimo, before the port, overlooking the big public beach where nobody ever goes. It was here, in a room with a view of the stone seawall that they had stayed in June 1989.

N called Niki was on her way to Ibiza, as usual in that season, and Claude, her husband of four years, followed, making the most of a short-lived resource whose origin he preferred to forget.

On this particular day N wanted to go to the hairdresser. In Barbès, where there are three hairdressers per street, she had acquired the odd habit of visiting modest salons and returning with elaborate hairdos of the 'permanent' variety. In principle, she and Claude thought it far better that she have her hair done when she was drunk; the results were really more spectacular.

In general, life seemed more pleasant to them when they had had a stiff drink. Thus they started about noon to run from bar to bar in Palma's poor neighbourhood. They had soon settled on a rather coarse local rosé. With the help of a few small carafes, it must have been two in the afternoon when Claude parted from N. She tried to find a hairdressing salon she had seen before in an alleyway that resembled all the others. Claude tried desperately to explain that it was siesta-time and that a metal shutter was probably hiding the salon-front. N was being unreasonable, drunkenness and heat clouding her judgement, and nothing could calm her down. They had a row.

This capricious side was the most striking feature of N's personality. Good company, ready for anything, she was at the time devoid of that slightly formal reserve, that absurd fear of staining her dress that characterizes the vast majority of girls. Though already slightly old—at twenty-five—she wanted above all to keep intact the inclinations of the suicidal girl which in the past used to win her some success. A taste for running away and self-harming, a voracity for disappearing, her whims, her edginess, contributed to her 'style', a kind of romantic personality. Besides, prostitution and the affronts endured by those so engaged, were grating on her nerves. N suffered quite a lot from this duplicitous intimacy, but could no longer step back from it. She gave Claude, and the others, the scene they expected, and that, of course, ended up tiring everybody.

Having returned to sleep at the hotel, Claude was awakened by N fussing around in front of the mirror. She was busy splashing oil over her body while dancing to Spanish disco. She had placed her cosmetics-bag and her transistor radio on the bed near the pillow.

Like all the personal belongings of a prostitute, the radio and the cosmetics-bag, in which she stashed her condoms, were somehow pitiful. Easily bought, easily lost, they were however the only treasures she owned in this world. When she left a hotel in the middle of the afternoon, at the end of a morning, anytime in full sunlight or beneath the rain, she bought something, trifles or more costly things: sunglasses, toilet bags, beauty products, female junk that she soon lost and was for ever replacing, just like a stain that a shower cleans, but in fact doesn't really. In Claude's eyes, those objects were sad. She didn't love them either but nevertheless prized them, as the price of her beauty little by little devalued. God only knows how much one can care for things one doesn't love.

"Honey, I saw the Hassan brothers. They're in Palma. We're having dinner with them. They're brilliant. They just arrived from London in their Mercedes. They've rented a boat. If we want, we can leave for Ibiza tonight."

The Hassan brothers were Maronite Lebanese who lived in the fast-lane. They had the eighth district style with moustaches at eighteen and their bottle of vodka at New Jimmy's. Claude had never thought of them as 'brilliant'.

"A boat? They won't be able to leave the port."

"Oh, you're so negative!"

They ordered fish in sauce, and Spanish champagne. The restaurant, Le Yachting, was overbooked so they dined in an old-fashioned establishment in the town centre, very dark and unfrequented near the Corso Alphonso–XIII, table seven, on the first floor, in a room with low ceilings and smelling of mothballs. The staff was old and all the waiters seemed to have been there forever.

Claude found the Hassan brothers transformed. Perhaps because they no longer wore moustaches. They were accompanied by an Eurasian girl who asked for Seven Up (because, as she said, she never drank alcohol) and a Russian they introduced as 'the niece of the dancer Rudolf Nureyev'. Niki pulled a face. Claude thought she was wrong: the company was select. A Eurasian girl remains a Eurasian girl, and as for Russians, one saw them less frequently than one does now.

The conversation was limited at first to standard views. The Hassan brothers were interested in the technical and financial aspects of human existence. Stereo equipment, expensive jewellery, especially men's watches, top quality cars and the price of exceptional real estate formed the essence of their preoccupations. Their main concern was to keep their distance from certain archetypes they had learned to despise through their contact with French society, especially a less than charitable clique in their opinion, the call-girls of the eighth district.

So, they insisted, at the risk of making their conversation tiresome, on the exceptional character of their car, emphasizing all that differentiated it from a mass-produced vehicle: the bullet-proof plating, the Pullman suspension, the souped-up V12 motor, in order—they believed—to avoid the devaluing cliché with which a nasty person like the Eurasian girl could have associated them, talking about them as 'the two wogs in a Mercedes'. The failure of their rhetoric was constant, alas, and the benefit they drew from it rather thin. At best they passed for 'the two pretentious wogs in a bullet-proof Mercedes'.

Like many young Mediterraneans of their generation, and especially the Sephardim ready-to-wear manufacturers they met in the Trocadero bars, the Hassan brothers admired the characters in Brian de Palma's *Scarface*. Alcohol made easier their assumptions of more and more assertive movie scum manners: slouched in their seats they stretched their legs under the table as they puffed away at their cigars.

"Did you know Diana's in Majorca? Georges, did you keep her private number?"

"No, Pierre, I lost it."

"I can't trust you with anything. You know, Claude, he damaged our car?"

"Whoaa, I was high."

"High or not, you broke a light and flattened a pedestrian. You really have to try hard to damage an 8mm thick bullet-proof Mercedes on a pedestrian, in Paris, on top of it. It was difficult. We almost didn't come. The police didn't understand what two Lebanese nationals were doing in a car registered in Texas."

"And the pedestrian?"

"Oh, I don't know, listen, he must have died, after all it's 8 mm thick plate."

The dull-eyed Eurasian girl became totally glazed, she needed sleep. As for the Russian, who didn't understand much French, she kept smiling without saying a word like some air-hostess in a sixties ad. Claude decided to praise the people who were about to pay for his dinner.

"You're totally crazy, you're really the craziest guys I've ever met."

He had almost said 'goofy' but remembering the dog from Walt Disney he thought better of it, for fear of annoying them.

Anyway, 'crazy' will remain one of the most flattering attributes of their generation.

Delighted, Pierre Hassan slouched still deeper into his seat.

"You hear that, Georges, we're the craziest. Claude, it's obvious you don't know our cousin Elie. You would really find him super-sympathetic, a real crazy guy. Once, he drove through Cannes with a naked girl sitting on his hood. And this girl wasn't even a prostitute but a real German princess."

Nureyev's niece burst out laughing, but it had nothing to do with the story of cousin Elie and the German princess. One of the particularly tired waiters had caught his foot in the carpet and almost fell over. According to her habit, the Eurasian girl, her head lent on her hand, made no effort to smile. Of course, the anecdote was not new. Claude had already heard it once or twice, each time relating to different people. Obviously there must have been a German girl who devoted herself to that eccentricity in Cannes in 1975, in Positano in 1966 and in Malibu in the 1920's. Since the story had been going round regularly, the countess had become princess or actress, had changed identity, car-hoods, but not her apparel. As for the driver, it was always a cousin or a friend of the narrator.

"And where does your cousin live?"

"In London, like everybody else. He works in finance. He might come to Ibiza."

On that pleasant prospect, Claude decided to go to the toilet. In boring situations, in a restaurant, nightclub or on the rare occasions when he had worked, Claude had the habit of going to the toilet for no particular reason, simply to escape from reality and his obligations to solitude.

He stayed there for a moment, standing alone, sad, not doing a thing. He felt like writing a poem on the tiled wall, one he had inscribed in the toilets of a bar sometime before.

Modernity modernity
Despite jeers and pleas
The lewdness of the debauchee
Shines for eternity

But he had no felt-tip. And that evening, the debauchees were neither lewd nor shining. As for eternity, it was rather badly represented by a half-dead palm tree turning yellow in the suffocating darkness of a small courtyard. Claude had discovered this nameless space on opening the toilet window to breathe. Within arm's reach, a withered palm was the same copper colour that old gold takes on as it fades. The suffocated palm tree appeared to him as the metaphor for his own existence. Tears ran down his cheeks. He was full of self-pity, an exercise of his talent which came naturally to him. Then he looked at himself in the mirror and recognized the handsome face of Luciferian beauty that enabled him to never have had to work, nor to make decisions and, finally, to have to do nothing with his life. He found himself still rather attractive despite the passing time, the wasted days and the lost years.

At twenty-nine, he had followed a declining slope, the light was no longer on his face though the shadows of time and the bad habits of life had granted him a slightly jaded charm. Delighted to find himself to his liking in such circumstances, he swaggered, and decided to face a destiny which was not his but that of a woman. On the corridor wall that led to the dining room, he noticed the framed photograph of a handsome man in a Lacoste polo neck shirt leaning on a Ferrari GT. The picture was dedicated to the owner of the restaurant by the Spanish racing driver Alfonso de Portago. The car bore the number 13. Claude remembered another photo of the same man, shot a short while before his accident. In the background, his bringer of bad luck, the actress Linda Christian, posed for photographs at the car door: parasite, dreamer, indifferent like a Fury before fate strikes. Linda Christian, Ferraris, death at the wheel, that's the real man's life that Claude would have wanted.

Viewed from the Mercedes of the Hassan brothers, night in Majorca seemed quiet and remote. Claude sat in the back next to the Eurasian, whose brown legs were as hard as sticks of wood. Little red curtains framed the door, as in those old sixties Jumbo jets that some South American airlines still chartered for their long-haul flights. Beyond the curtains reality appeared, and for some while that meant a canal whose banks they followed. Claude noticed the lamps of the quay reflected in the dark waters, filled with oblivion.

The Russian girl wanted to change her shoes. Her hotel was much more expensive than Claude and Niki's. It was located at the other end of the Paseo Maritimo, towards the marina, the bars and nightclubs. It had a seventies-style façade in glass and brushed metal. Above the revolving door, the frontage was decked with flags. The Hassan brothers and the Eurasian stayed in the car. Niki went upstairs with Nureyev's niece to see the bedroom and do herself harm by comparing it with the one her penniless husband had imposed on her. Claude waited alone outside under the flags that stirred in the night breeze. He recalled having met another of Rudolf Nureyev's nieces in Cannes, at the house of a white Russian boy, some years before. That one was an actress, and smiled less. The Russian guy was funny, he lived with his mother who owned a fast car which they would drive around in the hills. The boy had told him that one day when he was drunk, he woke up in the false ceiling of the Palm Beach casino without knowing how he got there.

Later, Ivan, because that was his name, had married Marina. Palma, Palm Beach, everything sent him back to the palm trees, one of which, a beautiful specimen, provoked the mystery of its crown in the grey and yellow light of the Paseo Maritimo. At night, when one looks at palm trees from beneath, one has the feeling there is something hidden within. A presence which would explain the sounds of human steps that palm-fronds produce when they rub against walls. And one even expects if one has some imagination, for a little white and hairy face to appear in the middle of the crown, like a ghost created by a spell. Marina's memory haunted him for the first time that day. Perhaps it was the unfolding of the evening which reminded him of another night spent with her in Paris long ago.

When they were younger, sometimes they used to hang around like this with older or richer people, dependent on their money, on their car, on their whims. Men and women who are bored like to possess a retinue of young male and fresh female followers that they can drag around all night and generally lead into their beds—though not always. To surrender to adult whims is a very reassuring feeling. One knows it can end badly but one lets it happen, and lets it pass. It's the resisting that creates problems, grief, painful scenes. When one surrenders, nothing serious can happen any more. That's why opiates, and most particularly heroin, are such formidable stimuli to such an existence. Sometimes the hazards of these escapades separated them. As they left a restaurant or nightclub, they didn't get into the same car. They were supposed to meet but in the end didn't. Either through the malice of a protector who wanted the 'little girl' all to himself, or for a more innocent reason like the drunkenness of the driver.

One evening, for example, they had had dinner in Le Coq hardi, a restaurant in Bougival, with a rather sympathetic couple. Their protectors were in their sixties, he was a famous art dealer and she a well-coiffed Brazilian, beaming smiles and very rich, according to the friend who had accompanied them. The Brazilian woman had spent her time stroking Marina as if she was a little dog, smiling continually, with the rubbery, soft and hieratic expression that face-lifts used to give to women. Her name was Simone, or perhaps Renée. She wore extremely high, thin sandals which accentuated feet as delicate as those of a Tanagra figurine. Marina was in the splendour of her fifteen-and-a-half years. Her eyes already shadowed by dark circles sparkled, and sometimes clouded over when the captive soul passed behind the iris. Those who give the impression of dissolving into tears at the same time as they laugh joyfully are very attractive, even for the most hardened debauchees. Simone (or Renée), once married to a film producer, was sensitive to that particular touch of the eye possessed by actresses like Romy Schneider and Ingrid Bergman. To see such grace

29

appear in a creature that chance had placed at her mercy gave her the desire to possess and, perhaps, but this was murky, to extinguish her. And also an old person's vanity remains juvenile even when they are rich—to exhibit the 'little girl' beside her as the beautiful trophy of a festive night. This drugged youth was spectacular.

When Claude and Marina entered a restaurant or an hotel bar, arms linked like two idyllic little shepherds, the flock of customers shivered, and a silence, as short as a breath, passed from table to table. Sometimes the voice of a person sitting with their back to the door and who, thus, hadn't seen them yet, continued to resonate in the room. But that solitary song faded before the draft created by the revolving doors had brought news of the arrival of the two children to the candles of the adjoining tables. The most ferocious denigrators of physical grace couldn't fail to notice the phenomenon which marked their every appearance together. Those accompanying them enjoyed the effect as an extravagance which made them noticed in the same way as a leopard on a lead, or a famous actress and all those types who guarantee a dramatic entrance into that brasserie on the boulevard Saint-Germain, this night-club on the avenue Matignon or on the steps of a theatre in the rue Montmartre, recently transformed into a club. A very young woman made-up and adorned, half-nude, like a walk-on part in a blockbuster set in ancient times, and a teenage boy with the stiff bearing of an aspiring Prussian officer, whose Amazon face could have easily borne the big black shako of the hussars of death, together evidently formed a remarkable duo who corresponded to the aesthetics of the time.

Seen from the Mercedes of the Hassan brothers, Tito's, the megadiscotheque on the Paseo Maritimo, whose entrance was shaped like a fake cavern in concrete reinforced in the manner of the great rock in the zoo at Vincennes, with access to its five dance floors on the outside via two glass elevators; Tito's that, for fifteen years, remained the place where all the youth passing through the island met; Tito's was still pretty quiet. It was only midnight and the Lebanese brothers, who thought Tito's was 'not cool', decided to venture above the sea front, through the shoddy streets where drug addicts, and bars for teenagers were to be found.

The big saloon car glided past clusters of girls and society guys seated on the pavement, motorbikes and bonnets. For one moment, as if it were a Pharaoh's chariot, the crowd closed around the Mercedes and even the fiery Georges Hassan had to stop. Behind the gloomy profile of the Eurasian girl, who, grey like a sculpted head, came between him and the crowd highlighted in the headlights, Claude glimpsed a violet neon inscribing in the night: 'Bowling'.

Finally they pulled into a quieter area, before the gate of an old villa which had long since been razed to the ground. Its garden was a waste ground, full of rubbish and scrap metal. In the midst of the ruins, while the car doors slammed behind him, Claude discerned the silhouette of a palm tree, the third he'd taken notice of that evening. Flourishing amongst the stink of the refuse, it seemed to Claude somehow freer, less ominous than the one on the Paseo Maritimo, and a lot less sad than the moribund mishap in the small courtyard of the Corso Alphonso-XIII. The only one of its species that had survived the collapse of the property for which it had served as an ornament, along with other plants. Behind its trunk, rough like an elephant leg, the bowling neon shone bright, this time seen sideways and squat. Three palm trees don't make a forest, least of all a dark forest, but Claude had the feeling that something or someone was sending him a sign from the distant realm of the dead—a frail apparition, still clumsily conjured up in the emanations of the garbage of the cemetery that scented the environment.

Agua Verde, the bar for the young where the six occupants of the Mercedes found themselves waiting out the final hours of the night, where the whole set of boys and girls with narrow hips would disperse on the urine-stained concrete staircases that led down to the seafront. Agua Verde, for the consumer drawn from the alley by the promise of small near-naked bodies rubbing together in the darkness, in the end only offered the disappointing spectacle of a gathering of slightly faded almost-adults. While the girls explored the room, the Lebanese explained to Claude that his presence was no longer required and 'of course' they would compensate him. As soon as she returned to the bar, N intuitively clung to Claude like an animal that senses abandonment is imminent. Claude let her. Pressed tight against each other for the first time in hours, they suddenly felt—shoulder to shoulder—the intimacy that unites those who have known and accepted one another totally. That maturity ignored by all—Claude and N were usually very distant with each other in public—they had taken to extremes. In witnessing again the gestures that passed between them in that short moment; they were the same that Orpheus and Eurydice would have exchanged in the realm of death. Claude quickly became ashamed of the caress, as if it was an intimate weakness. He withdrew his hand the moment Pierre Hassan looked at them. N's eyes dimmed and grew as cold as those of the Eurasian. That evening N perhaps lost the last bit of self-esteem she still had when, without any word of explanation, Claude left the Agua Verde and slipped away into the Majorcan night for more disastrous tasks.

"You, you're going to get fucked hard later on," Pierre Hassan whispered in the ear of Niki who had become his thing, and who smiled through weakness, sadness, and duty.

To reach the bowling-alley, Claude had to dive into a deserted shopping centre. The stairs, lined with fake marble, exuded the smell of chlorine, which suggested the presence of a public swimming-pool close by. As he descended, two or three times he crossed the path of young Spaniards going up to the road talking loudly in their incomprehensible tongue. On the third landing, a violet neon, a replica of the sign, crowned and lit two double doors with holes, like portholes, reminding him of the doors in cinemas and hospitals. The bowling-alley was open but its customers had left. He was just about to bump into the last stragglers on the stairway. The reception hall walls were decorated with stickers, the air, stale with human breath, sweat and tobacco, sole remaining trace of the vanished presences. At the back, a bay window allowed him to view the darkened alleys, their night-lights brightening the end with the miniature abyss where the skittles and bowls disappeared. On the left of the bay, between the cigarette-vending machine and a slot-machine, in a glass cabin decorated with sparkling stars and bats made of rubber, was the dummy of a woman dressed as a gypsy, her eyes agitated with their reflective glimmers. She was an automaton, similar to the one that used to have a stand, not so long ago, near the Place Pigalle, on the boulevard Rochechouart in Paris.

For a few pesetas the pythoness delivered a sentence even more mysterious, for it was written in Spanish, and a few rust stains made it difficult to decipher. On the small roll Claude held between his fingers, was written: *'Que se incarnamen todos t ... des ... '* It was more than probable that the word erased by the orange tears of the machine was the word *deseo*, which in Spanish meant 'desire'. Of course, though it was less likely, it could have been the word *desesperacion* which, one guessed, translated as 'despair'. Claude looked at the mask of the effigy, whose manufacture was close to that of the wax figures which decorated the private altars in Southern Spain and Sicily. Excepting the electric filament which produced a green intermittent gleam in the centre of the eyeball, the character's animation consisted of a mechanical movement of the lower jaw going up and down to copy verbal expression. That mute oracle, whose inspiration came to the automaton not from Apollo but from the crystal ball which she held in her hands gloved in black lace, resembled the reflex gestures of the suffocated and of fish pulled out of water. Then everything went dark.

The caretaker, thinking the place empty, had switched off the light. Only the night-lights indicating the exits shone in the dark. The automaton had ceased her convulsions until the next day. Hitting the double doors like the skittles the bowling ball promised to strike, Claude left her lair and climbed the stairs into the fresh air and sweet night of the Balearics where, if he was to believe the piece of paper he clutched in his hand, the object of his desire would soon materialize.

The Mercedes of the Hassan brothers was no longer there. N was well and truly lost. From a bar illuminated in red came the shrill and powerful voice of Veronica Spector shouting for the billionth time since the sixties the cool beat of '*Be my baby …* *ouhouhou … be my baby …* ' The vocal, it was said, was recorded in the dark as the very young woman who performed it didn't dare sing if the technicians were watching her; her singing shrieked piercingly like the song of some birds of prey that one can hear in September just before dawn. The stars of the north shone above the Bay of Palma as Claude went back down to the sea-front and the discotheques. The night breeze, light as a silk scarf, caressed his skin through the opening of his shirt.

That year the canon of beauty in terms of teenage hairstyle of the Paseo Maritimo imposed a kind of chignon-bomb, worn high, from which long wild locks escaped. Colouring was on the white side, or a very light Neapolitan yellow. Synthetic hair foretold the sophisticated pieces worn later, at the beginning of the millennium, by international artists like Shakira and Anastasia. Some girls who were more eccentric went as far as adding an artificial ponytail to their extensions. A specimen of such extensions tickled Claude's nose while dispensing the sweet fragrances of an American perfume which seemed to be Elizabeth Taylor's *Passion*. The little one shook her head as she chatted to her friends in the parakeet voice that Spanish girls adopt from an early age.

At the peak time—around two in the morning—one had to wait a quarter of an hour before being able to enter the famous cavern which served as a ticket-office and hall for the lifts to Tito's, the megadiscotheque. The three bouncers guarding the entrance wore dark T-shirts decorated with a mastiff's head, the mascot of an American football club. The print shone under the ultraviolet light and the three phosphorescent dog's heads seemed to have a life of their own, independent of the employees whose faces faded into the cavern's darkness. At times eyes or human teeth gleamed with a sudden flash when people who had passed the control leaned forward under the light to call to their friends still in the queue. The rhythm of passage followed that of the two lifts, there was no selection, everybody could enter.

Claude had been overtaken by a party of German tourists. One of the girls, a sixteen- or seventeen-year-old, had a tanned, expressionless face in which the eyes appeared set according to the prevailing standard (meaning on either side of the nose), though as if a slightly rushed job, like the fake turquoises on the Mexican belt she wore on her Buffalo jeans. The heaviness of her jaw, and her big flabby tongue, barely contained by perfectly sound teeth, betrayed a mammalian sensuality, of which her firm breasts, rubbing against Claude's arm, were the most outstanding features. Behind that specimen of the Bavarian race was an altogether more delicate creature. The first time Claude caught a glimpse of her, the darkness outside had laid beneath her cheekbones two hazy scraps which had hung there, digging into the orbits of her small bony triangular face, to the point of giving it the general look of a skull. Thanks to a move in the crowd around the entrance, two oblique eyes came up from the night and met Claude's, drawn by the attention he had given them. The rapes of war perpetrated by the Mongolian tribes on the East European population sometimes provoke, like here, the late appearance of some of Gengis Khan's horsemen amidst the Prussian or Slav families.

Claude wondered whom the young Mongolian-looking girl with the swan's neck and manic look reminded him of, when suddenly he remembered the strange little fairy that used to be at the Kaiser-Friedrich Museum in Berlin before the war. Her portrait had disappeared in 1945, probably burnt by the phosphorous bombs of the US Air Force. The work of an unknown painter, called, because of that one and only painting, The Master of the Little Dead Girl, it was sometimes reproduced in old catalogues from before the war devoted to minor works of European mannerism. Maurice Ben Chemoul, a character about whom we will have the opportunity to talk again, was in possession of an old copy hanging over his bed, and had recounted the whole story to Claude.

Another wave swept into the cavern, taking away the German fairy and her friends. Claude was stopped by security. The double of the old painting turned again, still in search of the interest one arouses in adults, as one is at that age. Under the effect of the black-light, her eyes shone white like those of an extraterrestrial in a B-movie. The Bavarian girl called her over to join her in the lift, and Claude thought he heard the name 'Marina' or perhaps 'Mina'.

Nine years earlier, it was on Simone's arm (or Renée's) that another Marina had passed security in a former theatre on the Faubourg-Montmartre, leaving Claude out on the street. She had turned back too, before being dragged in with the flow. Her eyes showed neither regret nor concern, only resignation, like that of N a moment ago. Girls were always the favourites of the rich. Most of the time Claude managed to meet up later. The repetition of a parting reduces its pathos but doesn't make it less sad, on the contrary. Bearing this kind of compromise without excessive emotion or involuntary outbursts ends by corrupting those who don't protect themselves better. So what? According to ordinary moral criteria, Claude would have been wrong to have not been able to protect Marina. But why protect her when such a stupefying weakness made up the essential part of her grace? There would have been some heaviness on his part to want to preserve a private bond, and on her part, to want to be defended when she was going out at fifteen-and-a-half virtually naked on five-inch heels. What a lack of allegiance to their style, and what an insult to Providence! If one is not capable of losing one's honour, if one knows how to say no, it's that one values the worldly things, for example, comfort, security, self-esteem or health. But only respect for God could justify the fact of taking such things into consideration, and God was dead for these children.

The impatient reader who might have become irritated by all these detours, as well as finding the plot absurd, can now start demanding some explanations about where we're heading. At this point in the novel, our duty is to give the reader some enlightenment. Our aim is not to tell him, or her, stories but to conjure up apparitions. This book also contains, in a minor way, the vindication of youth considered as the loss of innocence, in other words, the gradual awareness of its own exchange value, of beauty as it incites to disinterest, idleness and contempt for all merit, and, more generally, of weakness, grace and the lack of appetite of those who are aware they are desired. All of this in a world without God and without imperatives. It is thus the starry heavens, and that alone, which lights up this Satyricon in which the many characters only represent a few types, untiringly repeated: the little prostitute girl, the young pimp, the rich old man, the living dead … Their continual vortex will contribute to the reassuring moroseness of their encounters. Here, staircase-like reasoning will descend to the basement of the hero's conscience, similar in light and frequentation to the disco floors, and there, we will progress to the corridors of his memories still dark and congested, which will only lead us to the mirrors of his illusions, where the apparitions seem to follow one another without rhyme or reason in a slow theory of neurosis. In Claude's life, since adolescence and as the result of a broken spirit, everything has been a perpetual beginning, repetition, degradation, and, at the end of the account: sweet drivel.

And now that the general meaning of our *Anthology of Apparitions* is more or less outlined, we can rejoin our hero in Tito's, Bar One, in the big hall on the first level.

Like those nightingales that were once said to sing better after landing on Orpheus' tomb, the little German girl grew prettier as she stood at the bar a few inches from the unknown adult watching her. The fleeting grace of adolescence—everything that is called 'the beauty of the Devil'—increases as one approaches, not that it is made to be looked at closely (on the contrary), but because the warmth of the observer communicates an artificial fire to it. The covetous desire, of which very young adults feel the object, acts on them in the same way as those vaso-dilating drugs they will soon be offered in the evenings, drugs that will make the dullest eyes shine and the palest cheeks grow pink.

'Marina', or anyway the one called by a similar name, offered her admirer a lost profile, an attitude whose apparent indifference was nothing but a virgin's trick to avoid confrontation. Claude was staring at her, for fun, to chase her into a corner. The other girl, who was not so primitive, eyed him from head to toe as she whispered in her friend's ears things that made them both giggle.

They dragged themselves away from the bar and went to dance at the edge of the floor. The larger was jigging up and down with some energy, shaking her hips bound in turquoise, more or less in rhythm. Claude's favourite, lacking in confidence, was awkwardly stamping up and down on the spot, her head hanging down over a small traditional purse slung across her shoulder, the kind of tiny handbag usually favoured by tall, large women—a cruel favour for the smallness of the accessory only accentuated the corporal mass of its owner. Claude imagined the fairy probably had a strong and heavily built mother. For, until the age of sixteen or seventeen, the choice of accessories is often influenced by maternal taste. He thought about the ogre's daughter: frail and monstrous at the same time.

A young Spanish guy who obviously didn't know *Grimm's Fairy Tales* (though knew well the art of kiss-curls that he wore in a waved garland around his forehead like a sylvan crown) approached the two beauties, rolling narrow hips mounted on the long legs of a spider in the confident movement worthy of a hula-hoop dancer. Tightly tucked against his stomach, slipped into the belt of his black jeans, his packet of Marlboro menthols was like an invitation. The Bavarian girl who knew the world, sensed the opportunity straight away and projected herself towards the newcomer, finding instinctively the right gestures lifted from a choreographic vocabulary reminiscent of Madonna's first videos. Claude leapt into the fray just in time to catch the other one and, for the first time, looked at her close-up. She had a Lady Di haircut, a rough-edged leopard-printed T-shirt, the best-seller of the Spanish jean-shops that summer, a long slip which smelt of Ibiza's tourist market, and a pair of white cowboy boots which wouldn't have looked out of place in the outfits of Indra or Pia Zadora, singers whose singles she might still have somewhere in a cupboard back in her bedroom in the family home in Dusseldorf.

The girl was shaking her head from side to side, her eyes closed, absorbed in an enthusiastic—though in her case—desperate quest for the *beat*. Claude suddenly thought she had something of the look of Johnny Halliday's ex-fiancée, whose name he had forgotten. He vaguely remembered that that person (Johnny's fiancée) had preceded the famous 'Babette' in the star's bed, or, perhaps, had come just after. In any case, she was a blonde with a boyish haircut whose sole claim to fame came from a cameo in *How Did You Get In? We Didn't See You Leave*, a film by Philippe Clair with the American comedian Jerry Lewis. Only Ali could have told him if she was called Leslie or Beverly. Claude remembered having met her at an orgy in Ville-d'Avray.

One of the great classics in the free evolution of the dance floor consists in swaying from one foot to the other while moving one's shoulders left and right. Claude had thus opted for one of those rather sober figures which allowed him to touch the girl of his choice several times, that way breaking the famous 'intimacy bubble' that female modesty attaches so much importance to. The bubble was more fragile at certain places, like that strip of tanned flesh embellished with a belly button that showed between the cut edge of the T-shirt and the white binding of the slip from Ibiza each time the girl raised her arms in the air and clapped her hands. Where did she get those flamenco-influenced 'palmas' that disfigured a choreographic vocabulary that was already simplistic? Perhaps it was because she was on holiday in Spain? Anyway, that boldness gave the man the opportunity to touch the woman's skin, always a delightful moment.

To the sentimental reader who might rejoice at seeing our hero fall in love with a girl in a nightclub setting for holiday-makers, we owe a few explanations and a moral portrait. Of the two extremes of human life—ecstasy, more or less sexual, and work, more or less paid—Claude, like many men of his generation, but with more abandon and without the malice of many, would have liked to know only ecstasy, the illumination. And in the most trivial sense: parties, intercourse with women, alcoholism. And this without money. And though he was the least interested of men in sensual pleasures, everything regarded as a natural reward for a man sound in body and mind, he only accomplished mechanically, like a thankless task. Through a paradox of character appropriate to certain pleasure-seekers, he despised those who took real delight in doing rarely, what left him indifferent but which he did almost daily. Nevertheless he felt disgusted with himself for showing such little enthusiasm. Deep within, more than riches, women or favours, he envied the appetites of others, without this jealousy ever showing externally, for he was glorious with an affected indifference that gave him (especially at orgies) a look that set him apart.

Why then persist in this way? Because he had acquired the habit and, besides, he had to live. A pleasant physique and the instinct for partying allowed him easy conquests that he rounded up later for those, alas numerous, people who looked for people. Not that they wanted to make long-lasting bonds, but because lust pushed them to endlessly renew their sexual partners. In the holiday-resorts of the rich, they became bored like everywhere else, and wealthy holiday-makers appreciated someone rounding up girls for them. Rather than fetch the girls themselves, they liked the idea of having them delivered to their boat or their villa, in much the same way as pizzas or cocaine. Claude didn't receive much of an income for those introductions, but he was invited here, could borrow a car there, and gained some acquaintances.

It didn't always work out as one might have wished. Sometimes the young person was fickle or their modesty won over their fascination for luxury, and even the promises of compensation were not enough to seduce them. Unlike professionals who live off women, despise them, know and use their common failings, Claude didn't always know how to choose well and fashion his girlfriends. According to the real pimps, 'he was playing it a little too heavy on the romantic side'. Even if, as big Sam used to say (he was a scout for a famous model agency): 'A skivvy who climbs aboard a yacht worth twenty million must know what to expect', it was obvious that Claude was no monster and that some outbursts due to his disloyalty had left him with some bad memories. He couldn't help but be too sweet with his conquests and looked for a way to make each forgive him by pleasing them. So when later he would kiss the little German camper on the mouth, it would be above all for that very reason: to give her what each girl has the right to expect when she has permission to stay out till five in the morning.

Ooh baby come, come to my home
Ohh baby I want you to come …

Obeying the ambiguous injunctions of the singer Donna Summer, Claude and Marina-Mina kissed. For the girl it was a kind of intense moment, he felt her back stiffening beneath his hands at the same time as her tongue, not as pointed as he had imagined it would be, was exploring that cavern that so many

41

impurities had already soiled. Mouth full of saliva, of teeth, sometimes rotten. Mouth that had contained many filthy things. Mouth that had lied, betrayed, licked horrors and that, in the end, was not much different from the mouth of a virgin. For nature is coarse enough to let the soul pour out in a passage where it finds—if not the scent of the roses from Isfahan—at least a benevolent neutrality, since the need exists. Men and women's mouths are much like hotel baths, one forgets they have been used extensively when one requires them.

Outside the vault of heaven was overcast. Invisible storm clouds had silently screened the moon and the starlit sky. A tempestuous wind coated the surface of the sea with foam. The trees on the coastline were already shaking and everywhere pieces of cloth—sails, blinds, tents, clothes hanging from lines—flapped and puffed up with sea breeze. On the Paseo Maritimo a slanting rain forced the terrace drinkers to take shelter in the crowded bars, while the straw umbrellas, lifted from their bases, fell to the ground, carrying tables and forgotten drinks, smashing glasses and promotional jugs, and dispersing the colourful drink stirrers made of translucent plastic into the gutter. The headlights of the cars were reflected in the liquid projections, drawing glittering scarves in the air which plunged straight into the dark mud on the roadway. The hostile powers presiding over the destinies of holiday-makers each summer, and the benevolent guardians who, from their Olympian heights, saw to the enforcement of the moral law, had formed an alliance that night. That meteorological catastrophe disturbed the archipelago to such a degree that the local press pompously called it a 'mini-typhoon' and, if it hurt many yachtsmen, campers and bistro-owners, it saved the virtue of one young German camper as pure as the flower-girls of the Nibelungen.

No sooner had Claude slipped his fingers between the warm flesh and the elastic of the slip, curbing the jerks of his captive, than a German guy wearing a baseball cap appeared. Claude dreaded a relative (a brother perhaps, or a 'friend') come to save the family honour and he released his grasp. The girl seized the opportunity and stood up, a conversation started between the two. Claude thought he heard some elements of weather warning floating around in a flood of tragic words.

Turning his eyes towards the room to show a bold front, a kind of cool, he spotted, out of the monochrome greyness of the people dancing in the smoke,

That low and narrow forehead and those wide pupils
Of the passive beings loved by perverse Gods.

He wondered what the Eurasian girl he'd met earlier was doing there when she was expected as the Hassan brothers double-date. When she cleared a path and swayed towards him amid the dancers, it seemed like she was crying. However, the personality of that prostitute, as he had perceived it earlier, inclined very little towards the pathetic. It was at that precise moment that the camper leaned towards him to offer a goodbye kiss. As soon as she had pronounced the ritual, albeit slightly dry formula: *"Nice to meet you, take care of yourself"*, the girl was pulled away and the wet mask of the Eurasian appeared close up. Claude called her by her name (something like Linda or Vanessa), then realized his mistake: it was not the Eurasian, but Niki. The pain had disfigured her, erasing all individuality from her face, replacing it with features common to her race.

N blamed him in the simplest terms for having, without her knowledge, cashed in on her charms with the 'two bastards'. Claude lied like all people who think they are loved. He swore in melodramatic terms that he hadn't so far accepted that kind of transaction and that the Hassan brothers had, in a way, 'forced his hand'. Which was true. Niki left him, though not before calling him a 'pimp'. Which he was.

On the public beach at Palma, where nobody ever goes, Claude let the rain help him drown his sorrows through the night.

Before concluding this Spanish episode, we need to recall an incident that happened at the end of Claude's stay on the island, when he was in Valldemossa introducing a young itinerant beach-seller he had met in Port de Sóller, to a ninety-three-year-old Canadian painter looking for inspiration. Our hero was waiting for the business to be settled, reading the newspaper under a lamp. The old man, having suddenly decided to do his washing at two in the morning, was still to come up from the laundry-room. Claude wondered what he could possibly wash for he had always seen him in the same short-sleeved white nylon shirt. But the old guy was a personality on the island, having settled in Majorca as early as 1938. He knew everybody and it was better to be in his good books. The room at the heart of the house was plunged in a darkness that barely spared one section of wall where hung several souvenirs with which some old people like to be surrounded. In one photo he could be seen in the same sitting-room forty years earlier with his wife and the Windsors. There was also a photo of Hemingway and a hand-written letter from Chopin to George Sand. Claude, who had been given a complete tour of the museum, was now interested in the papers and especially a pile of *Detective* magazines of which the old guy seemed to be fond. An article called *The Disciples of the Devil* caught his attention. His eyes went first to the photos of things that resembled plastic basins filled with blood, then he read the adjoining text written in the sensational style particular to that kind of publication.

Under the police I.D. shot of a dark-skinned guy, he read a caption which disturbed him even more. *"Adolfo de Jesus, the Cuban Magus, Had already been Arrested in 1982 for Procuring"*. Without going any further Claude closed the magazine and hurriedly joined the old man in the laundry-room.

"Can you believe it, three pairs of sheets and twelve bottles of whisky in three days, not to mention the bath towels, all beyond redemption. That's the last time I invite an archbishop. Why are you laughing? Do you know that old bugger? It's Wallis who introduced me. He'd done her a favour in the case of the little groom the old queen had castrated."

"I lost my wife."

"The little Asian girl? She died?"

"No, she left me."

"Oh, that's sad, you made a nice couple."

"She left because she discovered I'd received a commission on her without telling her."

"You made a mistake, be careful, one doesn't meet that many people in one's life. When my wife committed suicide in 1952, I thought my life was over, then I thought I was going to meet someone else. It's been forty years, and I still haven't found another Yvonne."

"I know, but I did worse."

The other remained silent, as if he didn't want to hear any more secrets. They went back up to the room. The old guy closed a wrought-iron gate. It was a bit too new, and resembled Claude thought, the setting of a Zorro film. One would have thought one was in a Mexican hacienda in a B-movie.

"Isn't my gate beautiful? I had it made by the very last Majorcan blacksmith."

"Does it work against apparitions?"

"Don't talk about what you don't know."

"You know, I did worse than sell N, I sold my sister too … "

The other fled to the armoury for he didn't want to hear any more. At ninety-three, one has already sinned enough to burden oneself even more.

The day after, Claude entered a church and prayed, as he used to do from time to time. The incident remained with him for it ended in a grotesque way. The verger accused him of stealing the candles he had offered to the Virgin of Miséricordia, he hadn't heard the coins drop into the collection box.

HER NAME WAS PATRICIA and she was forty-two, which was altogether logical since there is barely a Patricia in France after the year 1958. "The problem with girls called Patricia," Ali said, "is that they resemble their name: they are quite nice but they look their age."

Claude called Patricia, 'Mum', as he did all the women whose houses he had slept at since N had left him, even if sometimes they were younger than him.

"Mum, where are you going?"

"I'm taking Jeremy to football practice."

Jeremy was her son, her real one. Ali's other worry, concerning Patricia, was that he didn't find her very stylish. First, her job: in order to impress she said she was a head hunter, but Ali—and anyone who cared to listen to her for more than two or three minutes—could see that she worked in a temp-agency in the fifteenth district. Then, her walk, that Ali compared to a Shadok's. And, finally, the way she dressed, which lead her irreparably into the same boutiques on a busy shopping street near where she lived, and everybody knows (Ali better than anyone) that elegant women do not buy their clothes in the neighbourhood.

When his old Arab friend Ali paid Claude a visit while Mum was at work, he inspected the CDs slotted in the columns conceived for their use by an Ikea designer, letting out cries of rage, Claude could occasionally decipher names with ashkenazic consonants like 'Goldman' or 'Feldman' followed by a rather disparaging qualifier concerning the artists, 'all Yids', or the owner of the records, 'a fucking idiot'. For, on top of his vices (pederasty, poverty, idleness), Ali was anti-Semitic and anti-women. He never really liked any of Claude's mistresses, except, of course, Marina and the famous Ira A. He had to admit that Patricia was not as good-looking as the others. But Patricia was good for Claude. Our hero considered her, in language devoid of sentimentality, to be an 'excellent base to fall back on while waiting for better days'.

'Pat', as her friends and colleagues called her, was never back before seven, a time when Claude always avoided taking his bath—for she loved joining him—or even to be home, for after a few months of being together, the first heat of passion having cooled, Mum's company had become painful to such a romantic boy. A forty-two-year-old wage-earner, mother of a child called Jeremy (like several thousand young French boys born after 1990), living in three rooms with a double living-room near the Porte de Saint-Cloud, didn't provide much material for devotion to such a dreamer's soul. He used to leave around ten to seven to have a drink with Ali. Their favourite haunt was a PMU betting-bar in the neighbourhood: Le Moulin d'Auteuil. Because the room didn't have a window to the outside, time there was suspended and the customers did not look like the residents of the sixteenth. Many old neighbouring racing-track regulars, a few women of whom one would have thought, without much effort, that they used to be prostitutes in cars around the Madeleine, one or two Hindus, a factory-worker in his overalls, some Cameroons, and a lot of drunks attracted by the huge counter with sawdust at its base like an ancient arena.

On the wall behind the counter was a television showing the race-results and, from time to time, other things with—for example—subtitles along the bottom quietly announcing: 'Coming soon, more strange news!' but whose promise was never forthcoming. The real shortcoming of this café was its toilets. Located in the basement, one had to ask the barman for a token in order to enter. Usually the light was broken and Ali, who liked to talk about that sort of thing, protested each time to the staff about the state of the place. What's the use of returning every day to voice the same indignation,

Claude thought. He tried to drag his friend to the Deux Pompes—a café-hotel situated nearby—which funnily enough served as a petrol station too, opening onto both the boulevard Murat and the boulevard Exelmans. But the shortcoming of the Deux Pompes—whose neon sign Ali liked for the various pornographic witticisms it inspired—was once again the toilets, whose key had to be asked for from the owner, and which were located in a corridor in the building and were not heated at all.

Why not extricate oneself from stories of toilets in the company of poor guys in gloomy cafes, when a tender and loving woman was waiting for you at home? Weakness was one explanation: for years Claude had the habit of submitting to Ali, whose authoritative character was becoming more evident with age and disillusionment. So he would have been wholly incapable of refusing a drink at Le Moulin d'Auteuil with his friend. To excuse our heroes it's worth recalling that this kind of behaviour constitutes one of the features of a man's soul. Some men will always prefer to hang around, even with a moron, even in the worst weather; initially with the vain idea that real life is somewhere else, then, once past thirty, through habit and boredom.

As for Ali, he had his eyes set on a sort of peasant boy from Normandy, found among the personnel, using the technical failures of the toilets as a pretext to get to know him.

"Come on, little one, move yourself, go and find an electric torch so we can have a crap!"

Of course the 'we' was, in Ali's mouth, a royal 'we', though a misunderstanding due to the lack of culture on the part of the Normandy boy, and the minimal majesty of the character who expressed it, could result, in Ali's eyes, in an excellent secondary benefit, in the form of a thinly-veiled proposition to go together to the lavatory.

After three weeks of this kind of 'circus', Claude and Ali were told by the owner never to 'set foot' on her 'premises again'.

So Ali, after having called the lady in question 'cow' and 'bitch', agreed to go once or twice to the Deux Pompes, then started to grumble at the idea of taking the metro from his place to the Porte de Saint-Cloud. Thus he failed to visit Claude, and the two friends lost sight of each other, both refusing to make the slightest effort.

Before that parting, Ali had brought Claude a book borrowed (and never returned) from the local library in the eighteenth district—*Christiane F: Autobiography of a Girl of the Streets and Heroin Addict.*

Although he had led Patricia to believe his head was 'filled' with solid projects, mainly in the field of women's hairdressing (this to convince her that he didn't intend sponging off her for ever), Claude had, as we've seen before, an imaginative nature—one that carried him more towards the realm of the dead, the dark confines of the Erebus, than towards the 'starting one's own business' section of the neighbourhood job centre.

One evening when he had had to perform a particularly tedious cunnilingus on his partner after which she had fallen asleep, snoring, leaving him alone facing the gloom barely breached by the light of an Olympia bedside light from Ikea, he opened the book with the laminated jacket. The iridescent beauty of Babsi, a dead fourteen-year-old girl, whose picture was reproduced among the illustrations, made his inner being tremble with love. While his inflamed lips were still permeated with the *odor femina,* the sweetness of a poetic emotion gave him the caress he had no longer expected. Babsi, whose caption said she was, in 1977, at fourteen, *the youngest O D of the children soliciting in Berlin Zoo Station.* Babsi, probably short for Elisabeth, was much more like the name of a fairy whose enchanting power one perceives only if one lengthens the first vowel, transforming the little word into a kiss given to the air, in the night and to those creatures that inhabit there. Babsi did Marina the best favour a young ghost prostitute can do for another, she came close to Claude and re-inspired a lost man with the sense of his true duty: to love, not merely to survive.

A sudden loud nasal snort emanating from the head on the adjoining pillow led our hero to remember the presence of his actual partner. He looked at that big face full of confidence and abandon, at the flaws in the pigmentation of her mouth where the pink of the mucous membrane had bled into the whitish skin like a blood stain on a sheet, the few blond stray hairs like pig's bristle which decorated her upper lip and the lower parts of her ears, the inside of her wide-open nostrils spotted with tiny bright red dots, her thick profile which made her resemble the potato used to advertise Vico potato mash. In short, having to pretend to love that creature, to lavish caresses on her, to feel her warmth, made her even more odious to Claude. She was not difficult to satisfy—after a certain age, people who live alone only ask for company and a few caresses which, after time one becomes used to giving without thinking. But in spite of that, one has to be interested, to give one's opinion on coats bought in the sales or ugly shoes, to try to be there, to take part in an existence which doesn't offer much charm. The worst being the surprises (always bad), the slightly mis-fired presents, the small vulgarities of the soul which come to light gradually, like the hidden defects of a second-hand car. And then the demand for love which is the mortal disease of that kind of relationship, the disgusting kisses, the scenes, the dinners for two, the pets bought together in a pet shop, and worst of all, the desire for a child 'before it's too late'. Patricia was not at that stage yet, but Claude knew the tune.

When he left the bed, the young woman stretched, opened her eyes and looked at him with a kind smile. At that moment, Claude felt like hitting her on the head with a hammer, but he was not very impulsive, so he returned the smile and sought refuge in the bathroom.

Like Le Moulin d'Auteuil, Patricia's bathroom had no window. The air was forever damp with the smell of towels and baby wipes. On the sink was a pink fluo hairbrush with a few yellow hairs coiled around its bristles. Above was a mirror surrounded

with bulbs—the kind one sees in the dressing-rooms of stars—
where Patricia had stuck some photos relating to her: holidays
in the sun with other people, a postcard depicting Marilyn
Monroe, portraits of the inevitable Jeremy, and, in the middle,
in the sweet and sickly dampness, something pink floated, like
a seraphim in the ether, a face which bore a resemblance to
a calf's head. On the top of the head, a few remaining hairs
showed, between their little dry tufts, the grey skin of the scalp.
As it had just resided between Patricia's thighs and the scalp
had sweat from contact with the *mons Veneris*, the tufts were
frizzy, like the pubic hair of the person we were talking about
earlier, by which they seemed contaminated. The eyes at the
same time dull and wet and slightly watering, questioned the
mirror, not wanting to admit the truth of the old adage: 'birds
of a feather flock together'.

Claude sat on the edge of the bath. He was not prepared for
such a spectacle. Another mirror alas, this time a magnifying
one, destined to seek out Patricia's blackheads, reflected him
in an even less flattering manner. He felt like breaking it, but
he made do with just turning it away slightly. Sadly he took his
calf's-head head in his hands. With such a physique, for which
kind of woman would he soon be expected to play the beau?
A school teacher on sick leave for nervous depression? An old
granny? Someone obese? Then even the homosexuals wouldn't
want him any longer.

He thought about someone he had forgotten for a long time,
a neighbour from the apartment in the rue du Caire where
he had lived with Marina. They used to call her 'the old girl',
she must have been about Patricia's current age. Claude hated
her, for once when he was playing his electric guitar, she had
come to the window, and shouted ironically: "Don't give up the
day job!" Her place was a complete tip, she didn't empty the
ashtrays, she let *France-Soir* pile up, and she was always in her
dressing-gown. One day, the ex-nightclub cloakroom attendant
had told Marina, speaking to her in a familiar tone for she took
Marina for a prostitute on the rue Saint-Denis: "Let me tell
you, love, it's lousy growing old." The warning, hurled from

deep in the past to a girl who couldn't have cared less, re-echoed gloomily now in Claude's ears. A tramp, that's how he would end up if he wasn't careful. Better go back to bed with Mum.

On some afternoons, Claude used to go for a walk in the Auteuil quarter. He had a special liking for the rue Boileau, because of a garage that specialized in bodywork, run by two Chinese, at the end of a dirt track which reminded him of a village of olden times, and also because of the detached houses with gardens hidden behind walls. At the top of one blind wall, above the cement roof, he could glimpse dry brown skeletons which seemed to signal to him. The following spring, as every year, the flowers of the wisteria would be reborn from that dead wood, allowing their tapering mauve clusters to hang down over the weathered stone, like young female captives who have been given permission to expose their arms to the sun for certain periods of time.

Sometimes he went as far as the race course. He would go up behind the boulevard Suchet towards the north and take the avenue which followed the track. At this time of year, at four o'clock, the immense sky and the fields beneath were illuminated like a gigantic *light-show*, enlivened with shades of yellow, of blue, of green and of orange in front of which, as in a Chinese shadow-theatre, the empty stands rose like the prow of a ship. When the temperature allowed, Claude watched the dusk slowly accomplish its work. First the foreground drowned in shadow while the horizon remained alive, then, like smoke breathed out by a great devil, the melancholic atmosphere spread to the whole of the visible world, only leaving a yellow line there where the earth met the sky.

Around five, Claude went home to the warmth of the dark apartment. He didn't turn on the light, or only the lamp near the sofa. Outside he could see the windows opposite and hear the Protestants from the rue Erlanger singing their hymns accompanied by an organ. These people occupied a hall on the ground floor of a modern building, and met to talk in a room looking like a nursery or a canteen. Then, before one knew it, they would go to pray in another room in the basement, one that could be glimpsed from Patricia's window, and the Hammond organ would start to play. Either one could see them, or one could hear them, but never at the same time, except for God, of course, whose eye went effortlessly through the concrete window boxes and the paving stones of the private garden. Did God like that music? It seemed unlikely. Or perhaps he had got used to it, like Claude, who tended to doze off as soon as they started, letting his book slip to the floor.

At six-thirty it was the rush-hour. He had to hurry to the Prisunic on the Place Jean-Lorrain to shop for dinner. Since Ali had dumped him, he had lost the habit of going to the bar or even of going out to avoid Patricia's homecoming. Some accommodations in our feelings proceed naturally from the submissiveness that age, lack of financial resources and the momentary fear of being alone impose on the most rebellious self. Those positive inclinations—which, you might notice, often happen during winter—make the person (who has them) feel real satisfaction in accomplishing chores that until then, he loathed. Ali was no longer there to bring that note of irony, that external look which prevented the crystallizing of positive feelings in a soul as fragile as Claude's. In fact, if Ali had seen his friend trotting along to the Prisunic clutching a genuine granny nylon shopping bag, bought at a hardware shop at the Porte de Saint-Cloud, he would have screamed in despair, like Ulysses discovering his companions changed into pigs by the sorceress.

Nothing definitive though in such metamorphoses. The return to a former state usually happens when the competitive spirit for change weakens. These new habits are all the more fragile for they are new and constraint plays a decisive part. How could they last when they contradict older habits which have the force of inclinations they have helped to establish? 'Claude the serving boy' (as Ali would have called him) thus had no chance, in the long run, faced by 'Claude the idler'. The latter would have avoided doing anything himself, but would leave the trouble of throwing the shopping bag out the window to another Claude, the more pleasant, 'Claude the virile', who would find it easy once spring arrived to rebel against degrading slavery.

It was not that Claude didn't exercise his virility elsewhere that winter, and with much brilliance. In the kitchen, for example, his desire for perfection did not allow him to become discouraged by clumsiness and lack of experience, rare, even in someone as lazy as him. With the enthusiasm traditionally reserved for beginners, Claude marvelled at managing to cook (for a bit too long) pasta with Laughing Cow cheese (one of his great achievements). Consequently, this dish, commented upon at length by its author during the ritualistic tasting, was the object of a true domestic cult of which he was the high priest. The dogma didn't tolerate any criticism, immediately perceived as a sacrilege or an apostasy. Patricia and her son suffered Claude's tyranny as they hung their heads over their plates. There were happy days (the Laughing Cow days), austere evenings, crucial moments when a smell of burning reminded the televiewer in his apron, deep in contemplation of the Telethon, that he had forgotten a feast under the grill of the gas-cooker.

"My pie is ruined!"

Such lucid outbursts were rare. Usually, according to a mental process the psychologists referred to by the term, 'denial', and which constituted, according to them, 'one of the conditions of the perverse personality', Claude formulated a rhetoric whereby the culinary served the soup to the pathological. Denial is saying the opposite of the truth while believing in it, without ignoring that this truth existed, which was a major difference between perversity and dementia. Claude used to improvise a speech all the more argumentative and long for the 'pigswill' (as Ali would have brazenly called it) was disgusting. Multiplying the unjustified assertions ('*Osso Bucco* always tastes like that'), never hesitating from handling the attack *ad personam* ('may as well give jam to pigs'), etc. The young woman endured the sarcasm with no other way out until the scene when the cook went beyond a certain limit. The bust-up happened one evening when Claude caused three nice pieces of boudin sausage with onions to explode on the gas-cooker.

Psychology forces us to unveil here a fact that our kindness has so far encouraged us to conceal. Claude's official surname (and consequently, Annie-Marina's) happened to be 'Boudin'. A difficult name to bear, but an old one that their father Bernard had received from his father François Boudin, who had inherited it from a long line of agricultural workers. Was it the symbolic massacre of those homonymous sausages or little Jeremy's screams? Anyway Claude completely lost it, threw his cloth on the floor, stamped on it and, after having declared to everyone and no-one, "I can't stand it anymore I want to die", slammed the door of the apartment but not before slipping on his coat.

As soon as he was out, he began mechanically to go up the rue Michel-Ange, towards the Place Jean-Lorrain, undoubtedly because that direction (the way to Prisunic!) was the one he took most often those days. But the more he walked, the less he thought about dying. Arriving in front of the famous Ecole des Oiseaux, two hundred yards from the apartment, he was already wondering when he could go back to Patricia's without losing face. On top of that, he had forgotten his scarf. Although only a minute had passed since the blood had boiled in his veins, his brain swelled with anger making his eyeballs bulge as they drew on a glaring blaze pushing from within, like the blackish lava of the over-cooked sausages that had exploded from their envelope when the inexperienced cook had pricked them with a fork—the nervous shock seemed to have finished its work, letting his body temperature descend a few degrees. But in the human brain, the damage done by that kind of outburst was not always immediately discernible. And the destroyed neurons, the false contacts, the mesmerism our passions impose on our chemistry sometimes provoke, following mysterious rules, after-effects whose symptomatology comes under psychiatry, if not forensic medicine. It is well-established that some criminals commit a crime after a row with their partner which, in another home, would barely have provoked a raised voice.

While Claude was walking along the pavement, two pallid-looking ectoplasms, starred with brownish stains like bloody rags, stirred on the periphery of his field of vision: the persistent image left in this soul tormented by the kitchen cloth soaked in pig's-blood which he had stamped on earlier, but also, and much more, the incarnate figure of neurosis and accumulated sorrows. Blood, loss of substance, dispossession of his virility, such were the morbid states whose standards were silently flapping around the head of the feverish man. In the same way the pigs of the Pontine marshes—poor metamorphosed sailors lost in the frightening animal night—must have seen in the copper reflections of the eyes of the sorceress coming towards them (whether to kiss them, or to cut their throats) the fleeing image of the degradation whose victims they were.

How can a cloth be metamorphosed into a young girl? Such is one of the mysteries that governs the destinies of shadows. Anyway, one of the bloody rags mixed with the other forming something which resembled a big silk scarf then, in a deceptive illusion, became the body mass of little Babsi who had overdosed at Berlin Zoo Station in 1977.

Dressed in dirty greenish jeans, with five-inch heeled sandals, worn-through and slightly too big, whose thin snakes of white leather straps imprisoned her fairy-like ankles, she was hugging her chest just barely blossoming with nipples sensitive enough to be painful in her promotional cotton T-shirt bearing the slogan *I've just come from Tahiti*; everything wrapped in a jacket of moth-eaten rabbit fur. Seated on a the hood of a car outside the posh school, like a forgotten boarder excluded for wearing the wrong clothes, the apparition was staring at her feet and the tarmac from under a chestnut-brown lock of hair streaked with blond.

For the reader who might suspect us of toppling into a ghoul-ish fairy tale or a ghost story, we'll submit a more subtle hypothesis whereby a pure and simple hallucination gives way to that embellishment of reality that accompanies certain mental deficiencies. At the time, the grand boulevard shopping areas were slowly being overrun by prostitutes from Eastern Europe, and it could be that one of them, one who was particularly young and sick, had got lost around here, in a state of hypothermia and drug overuse. Looking quite like a dead girl in fact. Poland, East Germany and some parts of Czechoslovakia harbour among their population, some morphologies more Saxon than Slav, and the young girl with the dyed-blond hair revealing an ovoid skull atypical of the brachycephalic race, could easily have belonged to the same Sudeten or Prussian ethnic group as the dead girl from Berlin. Sisters in blood, she was also her sister in fate.

The bloody rags, which had been used to build up the golem, or, in the perspective of a simple aberration—which had blended with the pale figure of the young girl lit by the moon—abandoned Claude, as if the fact of having to focus his attention on a tangible object had interrupted the flutterings caused by raised blood pressure. As a result (as happens to people prone to vertigo) the focal narrowing of his field of vision on a too-limited zone made him lose his balance. Leaning on the parked vehicle, to come closer, awkwardly, to the young person in rabbit fur, Claude slid to the ground. Until he found his head in the gutter.

Seen from down below, the still motionless young girl had taken on extraordinary dimensions. She resembled one of those ancient Olympians whose proportions and strength made intercourse for a mortal both desirable and dangerous. From her enormous white worn shoes to her small head crowned by the crescent moon which lit up the skin of her legs to display a thousand scars from blows, bites, burns, dark scars like those left by a whip and a few crusts of dried blood, she was nothing but a monument of wounded flesh. Her still eye, whose dark sparkling pupil Claude could discern from that distance, made one think of an animal.

The impassivity of the creature facing the man who had fallen to the ground could only be explained by mind-destroying drugs or by a feature appropriate to apparitions: their spectral nature prevents them from feeling compassion and concern. The marvellous being was not charitable. In this case, pseudo-Babsi didn't depart from the rule of her order. Nothing could divert her inhuman look from the tip of her shoes indolently swaying above the pavement. The moon halo deepened her features, making the oval of her chin heavier. She was becoming slightly more human and Claude, giving in to his fondness for comparisons, suddenly discerned a familial likeness with a person whom Ali used to see: Gloria von Thurn und Taxis. Same heavy jaws, same sensuality, same hardness in her pout. The resemblance was crowned by a significant attribute the German princess wore on the picture attached to the card the Arab had dedicated to her. On that polaroid, she appeared dressed as Artemis for a party. The moon crescent, emblematic of the Taurid Goddess, was suspended above her heavy blond head. However, the marks of blows and whip lashings, absent from the skin of the one, gave to the other the look of one of those child victims of a sinister tradition in which the oriental incarnation of the huntress appreciates the blood spilled by the whip even unto death.

As the little one straightened up, swaying on her five-inch metallic stilettos, Claude started to see her disappear and, simultaneously, to hear her heels clicking and the membrane of her soles rubbing against the pavement.

That's the end, he thought. And that evening, he sought shelter at Ali's.

"What life is this? Without a home, without inherited possessions, without dogs. At least one could have memories! But who has? If childhood was there: but it seems buried."

IN THE BARBÈS AREA OF PARIS, preparing his meal of leftovers in that dark kitchen full of doubtful looking piles, Claude liked to read. To accompany the onions frying in the pan, on which he was keeping an eye, he had placed a book by Rainer Maria Rilke on a music stand. Behind the cooker, the greasy smoke had yellowed a picture stuck on the wall from a fifties *Paris-Match* of the starlet Belinda Lee, Prince Orsini's ex-fiancée, who had died in a car crash. Screwing up his eyes, Claude could decipher the caption he already knew by heart, a caption which quoted the *Osservatore Romano,* the Vatican's official paper: *Beautiful and Scandalous, Belinda Lee met a Star's Violent End at a Hundred and Sixty Kilometres an Hour.*

Turning the onions with the wooden spatula, Claude thought that, although 'beautiful and scandalous' in his own right, he was not going to meet 'a star's violent end'. Having recovered from his delirious outburst and thus, separated from his ghosts, he was living like an old lady with a small pension in Ali's thirty-seven square metre two-rooms and a kitchenette studio. His eyes returned to Rilke's words: *What life is this? Without a home, without inherited possessions, without dogs. At least one could have memories! But who has? If childhood was there: but it seems buried.*

His childhood, a few Parisian names were sufficient to bring it back: rue Saint-Romain, rue Vaneau, rue Oudinot, rue de Babylone. The seventh district was not the same today. Except the Invalides, the Champ-de-Mars, the boulevard Saint-Germain and a few posh streets, there was a whole seventh that was more shabby. Blocks of apartments for rent, often quite mediocre, including two or three room apartments sold now for millions to suckers by estate agents, were at the time occupied by ordinary families. The *nouveaux riches* and the foreigners hadn't yet invaded the neighbourhood. Claude's father, a bank clerk, and his mother, a nurse, could live there without having to lay out the kind of rent paid by Americans.

Claude's favourite day was Sunday. In that neighbourhood full of churches and convents, in those streets already slightly empty each day, Sunday was a particularly lucky day. In the afternoon, they used to go for a walk as a family: rue de Babylone, beside the walls of the convents, as far as the Chinese cinema. Annie was still a kind of doll with blue leather boots and a navy blue wool hood through which two plump cheeks peeked. Monsieur Boudin, the father, didn't have a car and their walks, which sometimes took them as far as the Jardin des Tuileries if the weather was good, were reduced, if the weather was bad, to a short stroll in the adjacent streets, or a visit to an exhibition. Claude remembered the Dutch Institute near the boulevard Saint-Germain, where he had seen the Jan Luyken engravings that had frightened him.

These kind of people didn't own a television either and in the evening their father read aloud to his children. Before Chateaubriand he had read them Tolstoy's *War and Peace*, and several novels by Dickens. Annie and Claude were particularly fond of the death and murder scenes. Their favourite was the murder of Nancy, the little prostitute, by her pimp, Bill Sykes, in *Oliver Twist*. Annie knelt at her big brother's feet. He was killing her with the grip of his gun held at her temple. They were playing so well that both felt the warm blood spurting. They alternated with a scene from *War and Peace:* 'the death of Prince Andrei' in which Annie played the part of a military doctor who practised amputations and gave Claude a shot of rum. He remained stoic, staring at the sky (in reality a white ceiling, which had become grey with smoke over time) while she sawed off his leg with a carpenter's large saw.

Thursday's cinema was also useful in feeding their shared taste for drama. An American epic, *The Fall of the Roman Empire*, seen at the Le Duroc cinema, had impressed them because of some episodes that took place in the arena. A pantomime resulted, which could have been called: 'The Little Boudins Thrown to the Lions.' Annie played a young Christian and Claude the big cat. Covered in a man's tatty wolf-fur coat salvaged from the rubbish, the little boy threw himself onto his sister who was tied to the radiator pipe and bit her calves. After a while, the sighs of the saint created a miracle, for the beast, touched by divine Grace, submitted to the little girl and licked her hands. Later, Claude was astonished to discover, in Suetonius, that Emperor Nero used to play the same pantomime. Except, of course, he didn't stop at biting 'for fun'. Sometimes (rarely), they swapped roles, but Annie never gave in to Claude's injunctions and applied herself with a cruelty she undoubtedly would have liked Claude to exercise on her, in a way that would have left long lasting marks.

Incidentally, brother and sister were fervent Christians. There was even a time when they played religious people. Claude wanted to be a Trappist monk, like the Abbé de Rancé, and Annie, Saint Theresa of the Infant Jesus, whose hair she had seen exhibited in a glass case during a school trip to Lisieux. While all around them, a few steps from their Sunday walk, boulevard Saint-Germain and the seventies were astounded by their own boldness, these two children only thought about retreats and the desert. At the age of ten.

However that was not going to last much longer. One day as Claude was walking along the rue de Sèvres with a classmate, a yellow sports car—a Renault 8—stopped to let them cross at the traffic lights. Inside was a guy Claude thought looked very modern, and to whom he attached the 'pop-singer' style, and a girl whose hairstyle he thought was great. The handsome couple laughed, they looked like they were poking fun at the pedestrians. Thomas Poisson, Claude's classmate, said: "It's the hairdresser from the rue du Cherche-Midi. He's a drug addict." Drug addict, hairdresser, those words had been uttered in a contemptuous manner by that offspring of the Catholic middle-classes, contempt which Claude Boudin, poor and weird, had had to suffer at school. So he had an inspiration. Rather than play monk and nun, it would be sensational to play hairdresser and drug addict. Such a change of direction deserved, of course, meditation. He thought about it for a whole night before talking to his younger sister. Annie was very devoted to Saint Theresa, and she reproached him for his lack of consistency. For her, a hairdresser was the tall guy with a factory worker's face who, in his modest salon on the rue d'Assas, 'trimmed' their hair once a month. Nothing more interesting. Against such resistance, the erotic vision of the rue de Sèvres was no longer enough to sustain Claude in his new vocation.

It was Doctor Ben Chemoul, a child psychiatrist with a taste for little girls, who came to his rescue. At the time (1975), Annie experienced the first attacks of what everybody around them agreed to call a 'mental illness'. Part-time boarder at the Catholic girls school in the rue Notre-Dame-des-Champs, as the fifth year began she started to show signs of agitation which caused concern amongst the teaching staff. Convinced of having been chosen by the Almighty to accomplish a work of redemption, she started to deliver impassioned speeches that Mme Guyon wouldn't have disowned, and to make inappropriate shows of devotion such as to prostrate herself, lying flat on her belly in the bays of the chapel. The school psychologist advised her parents to take her to a child psychiatrist, who happened to be Doctor Ben Chemoul.

During her first consultation, which took place on a Wednesday, Claude accompanied her with their mum to the doctor's office on avenue Georges-Mandel, in the sixteenth district. The doctor's apartment was on the ground floor and led into a garden. Claude and his mother stayed outside, looking at the roses, while Annie had her consultation. (Claude learned later that Annie and Ben Chemoul had intercourse on that very first day.) In the waiting room, whose French windows led out into the garden, he was struck by the black-and-white photographs showing little girls all made-up with— it appeared—magnificent chignons. Today it would appear curious that a child psychiatrist showed such taste, but in the 1970's, people were 'broad-minded'.

The reader, even if he is also broad-minded, might suspect that that meeting caused changes in their family life. First of all, Annie left home for a while, on the doctor's advice. Where did she go? Nobody ever really knew. She told her brother that Ben Chemoul had 'lent' her to the owner of a tea-room who took her as a 'lodger' in his Versailles house. In any case, a few weeks later, she returned with opinions, vocabulary and manners that appeared extremely modern to Claude.

From the start she refused to wear anything but a pair of shorts in vinyl that a 'girl friend' had given her and which showed her curiously tanned body to great advantage, shrieking as soon as her mother wanted her to take them off in order to dress her in the Notre-Dame-de-Sion uniform. Out of the question likewise for her to say her prayers. And she no longer wished to be called Annie, but Marina. Their mother, in tears, called Doctor Ben Chemoul, who advised her to do nothing to contradict her daughter, whom he described as a *'border line'* personality to be treated with care. Their father made contact with the Jesuits in order to take advice from a priest. It was after Vatican II and the Jesuits referred him back to psychiatry. Another doctor recommended by the Jesuits, Doctor Pitoun, said nothing when he learned about Ben Chemoul's diagnosis, but advised them to try seismotherapy, very efficient, according to him, for the treatment of children with 'mental derangement'.

When the entire Boudin family paid a visit to Annie at the rest home at Yvelines, soon after the treatment, she appeared wasted, her eyes vacant like those of Aunt Jacquotte (an alcoholic with senile dementia). They understood, a bit too late, that seismotherapy was the scientific name for electric-shock treatment. Claude and Annie's parents shared a common disposition which consisted in a kind of fatalist submission to authority. But Doctor Pitoun could not convince them that electric-shocks, even administered under anaesthesia, could have anything but 'beneficial' effects on a 'growing psychosis'. So they went back to Ben Chemoul. Annie, or rather the one whom they were now obliged to call Marina, survived the electric-shocks like she had survived Ben Chemoul's first 'treatment'. As far as she was concerned, the only beneficial effect was meeting little Sophie.

At fourteen, little Sophie had quite an unusual experience of life. Her father had surrendered her to the hands of psychiatry more than a year before. Introduced by her mother to LSD and alcohol at the age of nine, knowing all the nightclubs in Paris, Mégève and Saint-Tropez, little Sophie was a kind of phenomenon (as Claude's mother used to say). Red-haired, made-up, usually balanced on high-heels, nourishing herself exclusively with cornflakes soaked in Schweppes, she bore the characteristic traits of those who will never age. She threw herself out of a window in 1979. When Marina met her, Sophie was on her third shock-therapy treatment and was threatened with confinement.

It was the Boudins who allowed Sophie to escape her miserable fate for a time. On a Wednesday in January 1976 she came to live with them at rue Oudinot, and from that moment, Claude learnt to lose interest in everything that in daily life diverts you from having a good time. Little Sophie arrived with funny little idiosyncrasies they had to endure if they didn't want to see her throw everything on the floor, or disappear. She also arrived like a baglady with several plastic bags containing all her treasures: wigs, records, photos of stars, and shoes from the flea market. She unpacked everything in the living room with a little explanatory comment for each of them.

"This one's for you, my little one, [she always called Claude that even if she was both smaller and younger than him] the white moccasins Alain Delon wore in Plein Soleil."

"Why don't you put on some music, Mme Boudin? No! Not classical, that's too sad. We'd rather have military marches or the New York Dolls."

Once everything was unpacked, she rubbed her hands together and announced to her new family:

"Why don't we all go down to the bar to pay a morning tribute to the canon Kir?"

After all, it was already ten o'clock.

When one is fourteen and tastes poison, one can't imagine life any differently. At the beginning one plays a double game, saying one's prayers, drinking Ricoré coffee in the morning with Mum and Dad and then, in the toilet, one swallows a tablet of Mandrax, or speed, with a gulp of whisky from the flask secretly bought at the Tunisian's in rue Vaneau. For music, it was more difficult. There were no Walkmans at the time, no record-player in the children's bedroom. One had to listen to the New York Dolls on the Dual Hi-fi in the living-room when Mum had gone out to do the shopping.

Sophie took an interest in her new family with the best will, energy and clumsiness of which she was capable. Everybody, even the butcher from the rue de Sèvres, or Abbé Billot who was in the habit of coming for lunch on the third Saturday of every month, was taken by her charm. Claude still remembered a conversation about the sufficient Grace (as the paper said about Ben Chemoul's Rolls Royce, that it had 'sufficient' power, without going into any of the trivial details of a technical nature) between the scatterbrained Sophie and Abbé Billot, chaplain at the Saint-Sulpice school. The Abbé defended the thesis that God gave each of us a certain amount of Grace sufficient to resist evil and be saved. To that Sophie opposed a contrary certainty that she drew from her own troubles. Nothing or nobody had ever been able to prevent her from acting badly, she didn't feel in herself any positive force and the only force which had ever governed her, was dragging her towards nothingness. Like every teenager, Sophie submitted her judgement to short term subjective impressions, but the colours she gave to her arguments were so dark and the images she used so touching, that they could only provoke, if not support for her paradoxes, at least a respectful terror in the face of such black certainties. As night fell in the room and the afternoon came to an end, Claude remembered having witnessed the tangible darkening of the atmosphere, the silence broken only by that childish voice which expressed so much fervour with such desperate words. Taking back, without knowing it, old ideas condemned by the Church, she re-established their efficacy through the total commitment with which she presented them. All ideas became beautiful and alive when one sensed that the life of the person who defended them was so engaged with them. According to her, if God hadn't given her His Grace, it was because He wanted her to lose her way, and thus, by losing her way, she was only fulfilling His will. So she had to lose her way. The Abbé, contradicted that her pride made her take for obedience and a mark of willingness what was only, according to her own principles, an inescapable mechanism. She abruptly cut him short, claiming that, on the contrary, she felt in herself a willingness to do evil, when in given situations at certain moments she could have done something else—and even more easily—but that that willingness pushed her always further towards her downfall. God had given her hands that she might steal from her friends, beauty to prostitute it, and when she threw herself out of the window, she would only go where she was expected to go. Those prophetic words which could have passed for provocation in a more timorous mouth, sounded like a stirring profession of faith in the complete darkness that bathed the room.

Cohabitation was short lived. Material reasons, added to a certain incompatibility of temperaments between Claude's parents and little Sophie, pushed the latter to end, after a few weeks, a situation which had become constraining for everyone involved. That lapse of time was sufficient to allow Marina and Claude to have two fundamental experiences. The first was incest—one has to talk about it finally—which was helped by the fact the fact that both shared, initially separately, Sophie's favours, heroin too, which Sophie didn't take long to introduce into the heart of the family home. Marina was very quickly tempted by the injections they gave each other in the toilet. Claude, prey to a rather masculine timidity (we all have some virile features), recoiled before the needle and was satisfied with snorting—a lot less traumatizing. Besides it was heroin which, because of its compassionate virtues, favoured, one night, the physical closeness of these three. They were in Marina's bedroom, on the little bed above which was a coloured enamel crucifix made in Russia, depicting Adam's skull at the foot of the cross (which means—I think—that Christ has given his life to allow man to come to life again in God's love), a skull which Claude didn't let out of his sight when his lips approached his sister's for the first time. It was Sophie who, through perversity, but also with that sense of relevance that the unhinged sometimes have, had wished them both to kiss.

That kiss, that insult to human laws, marked the beginning of their youth. The kiss was soon followed by the worst embraces to which they only returned (no more than four times) always 'completely wrecked' (as Nikki would have said), and always put off, deep down, by the stain of those gestures; always conscious of the stain to which they submitted their shared flesh, their shared blood. But everyone has to be young once. So, taken not by their senses, but by an aesthetic and lyrical vision of the world, they soon felt ultra-dirty, ultra-decadent, ultra-modern. In a word, ready for nightclubs and selling their arses.

Remember orange moquette
Remember my beautiful pet!

O N THAT BEAUTIFUL October day, Claude had opened an old shoe box where some of his juvenile writings were stowed, and was reading some of his best poems with Ali.

"This one was dedicated to Ira. When I read it to her, she said: "Is that all I inspired in you?" She was moderately flattered. She thought I venerated her like little Eric B who threw himself off a cliff for her, or at least like little Marc or the rest of her followers. Orange moquette, that made her think. But that was it: the carpet in the rue du Caire was orange."

"Did you sleep with her?"

"Yes, twice. On the 27th of November 1979 and once in January 1980."

"She was exquisite, right?"

"Yes, I suppose so. Though I didn't know her in the biblical sense in her best period. With me she was already a little bloated, with brown hair. But I adored her, she was our idol."

"She had brown hair?"

"Yes, the Alain Pacadis hairstyle, with a big hairpiece. Mind you, after that, she turned a very very strange Venetian blond. I remembered Nico telling her in front of me that she looked like Madame Pompidou."

"I love Madame Pompidou. She's my idol."

"Yes. But at the time, remember, it was not a terrific comparison, especially since she thought she was the new Edie Sedgwick."

"She doesn't look anything like her."

"Right, but in a sense, for us, she was linked to Warhol because of that film she made with him."

"You saw what he says about her in his diary. Not fantastic. He calls her, 'the fat cow.'"

"He's even nastier about Robert Mapplethorpe, Patti Smith and even Anna Wintour."

"Funny, maybe you'll see Ira again."

"God protect me from that."

"What's that poem? Is it longer than the others?"

"That's from a later stage in my work, 1983, the transsexual period. You remember?"

Wicked laughter from the other one.

"Did you write it for Kay?"

"No, Lilith. You haven't met her. She jerked me off on the Flash-back dance floor, during a Thierry Paulin show."

"The killer of old ladies?"

"Yeah, he wanted to be called 'Haussmann' at the time. Like the boulevard."

"Funny name."

"He must have thought it more posh than Thierry, for a lady."

"She jerked you off on the dance floor?"

"Yeah, we'd become friends. What I appreciated about her was her brutality. When I asked what she did for a living, she simply answered: 'I'm a prostitute.' Shall I read my poem?"

Shame. I didn't lose everything
each day swallows me a bit more
but looking into your blazing eyes—Lilith—
I feel able to throw it all away
—so fortunate is the abandon.
And now I pay attention to the sweetness of your tongue,
yours is thick like those of your species.
It's said you sin through your extremities:
so sin by the one which helps you to contradict,
O tongue which fulfills me.
Pressed against your scented muzzle
I am no longer part of this world but dragged
then lost
I am proud of myself on your account, little woman of the wood
and if I place my hands on your behind
it's only a formality: my place is at your feet.
For I will no longer see that oriflamme carried by you
From the adventurous kingdom to which I wanted to be devoted.

Benevolent scholars who might be interested in the poetic work of Claude Boudin will have noticed perhaps, set in the first third of the poem, a paraphrase from the antique poet Sappho: *'I pay attention to the sweetness of your tongue'*, a fragment of the famous *Poem to a beloved*, that Robert Brasillach, in his anthology, translated with restraint as '[Similar to the Gods the one]] … *who could taste the sweetness of your voice'*. Claude Boudin's 'tongue' is obviously to be understood in the sense of 'organ' but in French, from organ to language, as in the general language of caresses, there's only one word. Sentimental readers will discover that Claude Boudin knew how to show a soul similar to theirs, and that he was capable of lyrical outpourings which came—if not from the bottom of his heart—at least from an ability to adore, that only souls deepened, worked-upon and brutalized by a Catholic education, are capable. The idolatrous love Claude felt, at the time when he had written that poem, for some transsexuals, touched them for he was pure, like them. Fire purifies everything and that flame he saw in the eyes of his friends was for him some kind of Grail. Delivered to debauchees, they had no social hope; not even the dream, quite common in prostitutes, of stopping one day and opening a little bar, an interior-design shop or a beauty salon. They moved, dark in the solitary night, with no other future than the next day, like beautiful black butterflies. At the time, Claude liked to feel close to people capable of taking physical risks he didn't dare take himself.

But let's return to our October afternoon and Ali.

Who was laughing because he had heard 'extremities', meaning penis, and, strangely, the evocation of those shameful parts (or the fleshy parts) always made him giggle, he who had seen so many paraded in front of him. Claude explained that 'extremities' here designated first the tongue, which in men is less pointed than in women, then hands and feet traditionally supposed to betray the true nature of those beings, and then, of course, the penis that the most interesting of them retain at the same time as they grow breasts.

Ali was looking through the window at the sandwich-seller, a Maghrebi who, at the street corner, was producing fake *chewarmas* with French *baguettes*.

"I'd like a sandwich."

Ali, who always obeyed his impulses, went down to buy himself a sandwich and Claude stayed alone with his shoebox full of old yellowed papers and Photomat images from the heroic period. Some photos were still in a strip. Because of their better sense of contrast, Claude preferred those black and white strips of three that one could have done at the time in the photo-booth on the boulevard Raspail, level with the Alliance française. There was a series with Marina and Sophie, another with little Marceline, a friend at the time, one with Ira A, unfortunately slightly washed-out. A last series, that Claude considered among the best, showed him between a couple he didn't recognize. It came from Marina's stuff. He couldn't put a name to them. The girl, a brunette with frizzy hair who looked like Gaëlle or little Valerie, had her eyes wide open and was wearing a Snoopy badge. As for the boy, a brown-haired dandy with heavy eyelids, he looked like little Marc though more vulgar, but it was not him. Who were those people? A mystery. Perhaps Ali would know. If those pictures made Claude so happy, it was above all because he thought he looked superb in them. A very vampiric beauty, a very fallen angel. When he was sixteen, he was amazed by photos of himself. He gazed at them endlessly, and each time the little latticed orifice of the Photomat spat out its verdict, he was impatient to see the confirmation of that delightfully unfair gift of nature. The greatest unfairness perhaps. The same pleasure he felt when he started up Ben Chemoul's Rolls Royce on the Place du Trocadéro, and saw the old pretty-boys pulling faces. He had the Rolls, the physique, and he hadn't done anything to deserve it. No fraudulent transaction, no tax evasion, no boring pharmacy studies. He was an incompetent, not even a real guy, but the devil was his friend. Afterwards, when everything had collapsed, he discovered, with bitterness, that even ordinary people, the 'hideous ones' (as Niki used to say), had at least one photograph of themselves in which they were incredibly sublime. Never mind that they had cheated, had thrown away those where they were ugly. He had lost plenty, but he was above all handsome, and this one, with the two unknowns, was the best. He felt once more the magic working on him, the divine breath of narcissism reinflate him like a drug-high.

He put David Bowie's *Let's dance* on the battery-operated ghetto blaster and danced alone in the thirty-seven-metre square-two-room studio in front of grimy windows, trampling old stuff, love letters, ex-fiancées' photos, the tail of Ali's cat which fled to the stinking kitchen … He was so carried away that he didn't hear Ali drumming on the door with his *chewarma* oozing with 'home-made' chips and two cans of Gini soda. Always generous, Ali had probably spent his last five francs to buy him that disgusting beverage. Always second degree (Claude thought Ali was perfectly capable of second degree agonizing), the crazy Arab howled "Gini Gini", laughing and dancing a kind of French cancan to David Bowie, while biting into his baguette.

"Let's dance yeah yeah. Let's dance!!!"

At fifty-two, it wasn't bad. Milosevic, the neighbour downstairs, a Yugoslav whose name was a homonym of his Serb president, used his broom to express his disagreement. Claude lowered the volume immediately. Ali was furious for he enjoyed loud music, and also loved arguing with the neighbours. Claude not. To calm the beast, he showed him the splendid Photomat image. Ali scratched his old hair-piece, under which he hid his baldness, like Poivre d'Arvor the television-presenter.

"I don't know her. Never seen her. But him, he's 'the Cuban'. A horror who used to fleece gays. Never knew his name. He was always at the Mudd Club in New York with Tina L'Hotsky. I think he went out with Ingrid Casarès later. He looked like a porn-star whose name I've forgotten. Terrible states he used to be in. Always had a knife in his pocket that he enjoyed taking out. He was six feet tall. Perhaps you didn't know him. He came to Paris sometimes, always with Tina, always wearing Mexican boots with metal tips."

"Obviously I knew him. Since I'm in the photo with him."

Ali burped in Claude's face, letting out a smell of old onion spiced with Gini.

"Hey, it's not you there! It looks like an angel."

"Wait a minute, bitch, when you met me, I looked like that."

"That's true, you were as pretty as a girl. But here you are different, you don't look like you. No, it's not you … "

At first, Claude thought Ali was saying that to make him mad. But examining the Photomat closely, he was forced to accept the upsetting truth: the best photo of himself he possessed was not a photo of him, but of another guy.

Ali went further.

"Look at the stamp on the back. It's an American Photomat."

Claude hadn't been to America before 1985.

They didn't have the time to figure this out. For Ali, his chips barely chewed, was suddenly impatient to go to the Elysée-Montmartre for a ready-to-wear fashion show; Ali was so disconnected after thirty-five years of debauchery that desires streamed into his head, as brutal and hurried as the immigrant workers in the slaughter houses which not so long ago were a Barbès and La Chapelle speciality, and the hotel, now frequented by junkies—which faced his studio—whose Restoration façade with its two dirty cherubs in the roundel above the half burnt main entrance reminded him of the outside world. It's typical for some ageing male homosexuals to have no recourse against the demons which come to taunt them, with less violence than when they were twenty, but with the nauseating certainty that they hold their prey fettered and submissive, so much so that a single small grinding of their chain, a vague tug at the collar, the shadow of a pretty-boy on the wall, is sufficient to encourage those unfortunates stricken by exasperation to throw themselves against the fleeing apparitions who brandish before their eyes the malicious force which gorges itself on their remains. Such are the damned, without, nevertheless, what little that was left of awareness which allowed Ali to appreciate still the smell of a rose, the taste of a *chewarma,* the beauty of a child or of a dead Christ. That half-zombie hadn't yet entirely lost the battle against the forces of evil, but let's say, in conclusion that it was off to a bad start.

The ready-to-wear show advertised for seven o'clock wouldn't start before eight, but Ali felt like having a beer at Les Oiseaux, where he hoped to meet up with some old acquaintances.

When they arrived at the Arab bar, they came upon N, a former editor-in-chief who announced to Ali the news of her come-back on a 'big project'. Her thundering self-confidence was tempered by the greasy face, damp eyes and a small dripping at the corner of her lips which betrayed an alkaloid addiction of the red wine type. If it were not for her striped trousers and her accessories, N would even have resembled one of those female tramps who, in the company of men, quench their thirst with a little glass of rum in the bars of Paris. Fair game for the maggots of the Thiais cemetery, where the poor and unknown are buried. But N was not ready yet. Always in search of a drink or an arm to brush with her flaccid fingers, she considered herself not a young hope, but a 'sure thing', 'one of the two or three women in the whole of Paris, whom the advertisers are ready to follow'. Meanwhile, she went down to the toilet where, as Ali couldn't refrain from remarking loud and clear, "nobody followed her".

Next to them stood Edward, a kind of Englishman with discoloured hair and a nero fringe. He had the demeanour of a simple and honest boy with red cheeks, the sporty type who is not, in principle, interested in the affected ways of homosexuals. The funny thing was that he was everywhere, in all the places where homosexuals were, like a watchman in a designer-suit, at every fashion show, every backstage, every meagre party that milieu still agreed to offer journalists. Claude remembered a visit to Barbès when, having arrived with Ali and a six-pack of Kanterbrau, Edward, at the time an employee of LVMH, had gone on and on about his salary (65,000 francs a month in 1997), going as far as to drag them onto the balcony to show them his company car, an unlikely Ford Orion coupé in a metallic mauve, a colour usually reserved for rented cars on which the sellers of fake Lacoste shirts from the stolen goods market displayed their wares. Since then, Edward had lost all privileges, was living solely on his freelance work, and drove an old Solex 2000, which, in fact, was doing him good. He was definitely more cool, more 'alcoohol', as Ali said.

Ali, a former young hopeful of design, preserved by drugs and bad company from the easy bitterness of success, remained surrounded with a halo of some kind of legitimacy, that his failure rendered inoffensive. His words could still cork a few holes between two more useful conversations. Claude, obscure and not particularly a man of the world, used to hide behind Ali, but he suddenly found himself among family: Medora, a tall girl with a strong jaw, rather beautiful, had come to join their little circle. Claude said hello to Marina's daughter, who responded with a nod. He noticed that the bottom of her trousers, somewhat rigid, which totally covered the four-inch stiletto heels of her Manolo Blahnik shoes bought in London for at least £500 were dragging on the floor of the bar, sweeping up the fag ends and the spit of the Arabs. He would have loved to have seen the arch of her foot and the delicate small veins filled with young blood, the Boudin blood curiously mixed with that of the Romanov's, caressed by the wet and dirty threads of her badly cut designer-trousers which were baggy at the crotch, as if she was wearing nappies. But for that she would have had to sit on a leatherette bench, as was proposed to her by the bisexual Arab dealers with their charcoal eyes blackened with kohl, who made obscene gestures while eyeing her elegant posterior.

Medora was obviously not looking in the direction of these sub-humans and was only addressing N, the former journalist while brazenly ignoring her Uncle Claude and Ali. Claude knew her little white teeth, which seemed completely fresh, and from which escaped a volley of fast sentences, full of precise tongue-tip articulations—pronounced like a snob—which allowed him to glimpse that other old friend, a tongue pink and cold like a baby snake's, the tongue of the little girl she once was. More than her spiteful arrogance, which could have seduced Claude, what kept him at bay was the slightly putrid smell that emanated from that little girl mouth, 'a real dog's breath,' our hero thought, stepping back a little. A gesture Medora mistook for an invitation to move closer to N, shoving him shamelessly, as she probably did in the press sales or at the entrance to fashion shows, to reach what she coveted: here information which could help her advance a pawn to manoeuvre herself into one of those consultant's jobs they all had the ambition to hold, or to prevent a rival from obtaining it. Entirely taken by a quest which made her insensible to the heap of spit she still continued to trample, like a lyre-bird looking for its meal in a cesspool, she moved her small head forward in a menacing manner above that of the false tramp whose frog's mouth, split wide, opened and closed as a reflex effect, without for all that, nourishing her.

Moved by an ill-considered desire to be visible in the eyes of the lyre-bird, Claude said something. Immediately four small piercing eyes settled on him. Those of Medora quickly turned away, for she didn't give any value to her uncle, and returned to peck at the same old rottenness. The other look came from a pig. Dressed in a de-structured black suit covered with spit or with sperm (depending on where the spots were), he edged his way towards Claude and started to court him by stroking his arm. Ali, ousted by Medora and feeling suddenly confident among sure friends, decided to share with them one of the fleeting poetic impressions that were his speciality.

"N is nothing but an old bag of shit."

It was said loud enough for N and Medora to hear.

Ali saw the piglet step back, to avoid receiving his spit, but also from being dragged into a compromising conversation. Ali moved forward one step.

"She called me the other day to ask if I knew a place 'big,

dark and slightly dirty to organize a show'. Do you know what I answered?"

Sensing a horror coming, the other tried to back off but curiosity and the column at his back prevented him.

"I told her: 'Yes I know one, Thierry Mugler's asshole!' "

Ali's voice had risen as if in a crescendo at the opera and the words 'Thierry Mugler' and 'asshole' resounded in the bar filled with spies. The guy in front of him nearly fainted but Ali grabbed his victim by the sleeve.

"Well, I'm sure she repeated it to the interested party, which, in any case, between you and me, leaves me completely indifferent. Don't you think I'm right?"

In a faint voice, as if to make a counterbalance to the effect of Ali's yelling, the other murmured:

"You think so?"

Attracted by what she'd heard about the anal cavity of a designer on whom she was preparing an hagiography, an ageless pen-pusher with ginger hair and a sheet of plain features, passed within reach of the piglet who threw himself into her arms.

Ali, who never enjoyed it as much as when he had succeeded in compromising someone—as if the disgust he inspired replaced the desire of which he had once been the object—smiled to the company at large, with malicious eyes, suddenly young and bitchy, like the little rascals from the streets of Manilla he used to seduce with one or two francs when he still had the means to afford charter flights.

Claude took the opportunity to come closer to his only relative, who was on her mobile phone, and turned away as he approached. With no embarrassment whatsoever, for Medora was not looking, he examined her long white hand placed, as in an arabesque on her dark clothes, in the manner which the old painter Boldini, in 1900, liked to position his models. He continued up to the profile where the short and straight nose disappeared behind the hill of a still chubby cheek: a Watteau. Claude thought about his sister of course, whose fate Medora overtly claimed not to be the slightest bit bothered about—"I am Romanov enough and hardly at all a boudin", she used to say—he also thought about Watteau's shepherdesses, long dead, Boldini's models who nourished, like Cléo de Mérode, a few yew trees in the cemetery, people in car crashes like Belinda Lee and the formidable contingent of fresh flesh that beauty provided year in year out, an army as inexhaustible as that with which Stalin diluted the German front line, and whose every recruit ignored even the name of the one who preceded her. All these apparitions, sometimes trembling, sometimes pushed to the archetype, sometimes only known to their neighbours (like the fairy of Palma de Mallorca), sometimes famous, all dead, all forgotten. This common measure, this lack of hope gave the grace of an adornment to the arrogance of the tall snobbish girl. What suits a person best is what is natural, but doesn't belong except in an ephemeral way, such as that sudden preoccupation which makes her frown and raise her voice with no sense of discretion whatsoever for those nearby who could hear everything she was saying—according to the habits of this particular milieu where it's a sign of baseness to speak in a low voice:

"Listen, Sophie-Charlotte, if you're sulking, it's not my problem … " Her tone of voice contradicted the meaning of the message: it seemed on the contrary that the argument with the aforesaid Sophie-Charlotte was indeed Medora's problem, a preoccupation which for the moment took up her entire predatory attention, but which, if one mentioned it later, would arouse no memory whatsoever. The futility, the ephemeral nature of her existence contributed to the essence of her seductiveness not only in other people's eyes but in her own—not that she had a clear awareness of that lack of balance but because it was precisely that lack of balance which made her attach so much importance and devote so much effort to things that she would forget the very next day.

It was to the inconsistency of her inner being that she owed that beautiful wild animal energy, that sense of craving. Intensely present, realist to the point of being dishonest, dishonest to the point of violence, a violence forbidden by her purely conventional sense of morality, attentive but insensitive,

78

intensely vain but equipped with a self-esteem so inured to all sorts of wounds that no baseness could discourage her, and with that charming, cajoling, child-like, capable of paying the sweetest attentions to whomever male or female was useful at that moment, then suddenly with the same person entirely cold, hard, shamelessly brutal—wasn't she saying to her assistant, whom the night before she had called 'sweetie'—"One day your father is dying, the next its a painful period, there's always a good reason to take time off. I'm fed up with you." And everything that touched so-called natural feelings, like the love of one's children, was childishly artificial to the point of appearing ironic. Claude could see her showing the photo of her two-year-old daughter (allegedly the natural child of the billionaire Donald Trump) to a brain-dead fag, shrieking in his ear: "Oooh, isn't she a little cutie!?" using a standard phrase, borrowed from the world of sentimental clap-trap which amused her.

Everything came together to form a beautiful nature perfectly adapted to its milieu which, in attempting to summarize its complex magnificence, some—like Ali—might define simply as: a heartless cunt.

As Medora was rushing past him to throw herself into the arms of an old lady in leather trousers, Claude went out alone onto the pavement. He decided to walk along the boulevard Rochechouart towards the old Médrano Circus, in the past called Boum Boum Médrano, after the famous clown.

Having reached the rue des Martyrs, whose name sent him back to his early vocation, that which he had shared with Marina and that perhaps she alone had accomplished, he smelt the smoke of a wood-fire, as happens sometimes in Paris in the autumn. The desire to extricate himself from this world, to leave for the countryside, aroused an old ache. He thought about the Algerian woman leaning on the arm of a Negro who, precisely here, had approached the poet Saint-Pol Roux. "Go to Camaret, that's where I was born," a mysterious order which

Saint-Pol Roux could only obey. As Claude didn't have the means to buy a manor-house, and could barely afford a train ticket for Brittany, no apparition of that kind had ever modified the course of his existence. He regretted it.

The old Médrano Circus had been replaced by a Shopi cafeteria. Claude and Annie had spent delicious moments at the Médrano sniffing lions' pee backstage while visiting one of their Mum's woman friends who was an animal trainer. At the time Claude favoured Italian trapeze-artists and particularly a rather plump blond, whose blue and silver leotard and white leather boots, impervious to the sawdust soaked with piss, seemed to him wonderful attributes. She was probably dead now, or looked like the transvestite Coccinelle. At the time, she flew in the red-black heavens of the now defunct Médrano to the accompaniment of the circus band, and the boum-boum-boum of the drum announcing the high point of the act, a perilous triple somersault that she didn't perform any longer—for she was too heavy now for that—but that a young girl in her troupe, dressed similarly, successfully performed every evening and every Sunday afternoon in a deathly hush. Claude's eyes had met hers only once. Still dripping with sweat, pushing back a tiara that had slid down during her last somersault, she had given him a glimpse of her shaven armpits, full, rounded like those of the plump young fillies spread out on the pages of *Playboy*. That was all, but it was enough to make him dizzy.

Backstage, where he was now making his way with Ali, he was no longer so impressed by the artists. He still paid attention to the kind of trapeze-artist that any beautiful girl had become for him these days, but such encounters didn't fire him with enthusiasm, especially, to be honest, since the time when they were no longer successful. What he took for an aversion to the world and which was perhaps only the result of the indifference of the world towards him, had thrown him into the failings common to shy or embittered people: a vague religiosity mixed with an intense feeling of love for the countryside. He found in the whole of nature, where the inner self—in the past the sole object of his emotions—had dissolved, a real counterpoint to his melancholy. As the old man watched out for the first signs of the return of spring, the old beau, abandoning the art of portraiture for that of landscape, embraces with delight material things, but all he is doing is pushing back the limits of his self-esteem. Resolving without repenting, desiring that things be larger and more beautiful than ourselves, the rapture in which the new convert finds himself, serves only to reinforce the feeble weakness with which the process began.

The best moments in Claude's life, since the disappearance of his madness, could be summed up as long walks in the park of V or the woods near Senlis, a Swiss lentil soup cooked on a gas-ring, and the never-ending reading by the light of the orange street lamp the Paris authorities had placed just above his bedroom window.

As for Caroline Choukroun, she didn't like the countryside. When Claude passed the girl the American press had labelled *La Parisienne* on the stairs of the Elysée-Montmartre, he thought about the social divide that separated him from the yellow-eyed girl who had frequently visited, like him in 1976, another Elysée (the Elysée-Matignon of the deceased Armel Issartel, who died of Aids in prison, according to Ali's card) and occupied now such a superior position that she couldn't imagine how people she once knew in the past could look like tramps. In the past, Claude had had dinner at her place in Alma, with Ali. As they were leaving the dinner, the Arab, after roughly estimating the rent, remarked to Claude that they and Caroline Choukroun hadn't taken the social elevator in the same direction.

On the stairs of the Elysée-Montmartre, on the other hand, the two friends overtook *La Parisienne* and her followers, and suddenly Claude caught sight, at the top of the stairs, of the ageless, soulless mask of a forty-year-old young lady, N called Niki, who had loved him, so dearly, him, Claude Boudin and no other. The visitor from the past was leaning against the railing, talking with an ultra-skinny red-headed Englishman and a peroxide blond with a crackpot smile. The red-head waylaid Ali, and Claude fled through the revolving doors to escape the confrontation, filled with regret for those arms he missed so much. But it was too late. Thus life obliges us to betray our most intimate desires, because—we'd like to think—of a last minute scruple, a passing timidity provoked by the sudden appearance of the one we loved, a new expression we didn't recognise or simply because of the presence of someone at their side. But in reality we know very well that the given moment when everything was still redeemable is over, nor is it possible to establish when that mysterious interdiction was pronounced. Claude was not indifferent to Medora's contempt—he was used to it—but N's coldness, when he hadn't seen her since that night in Palma, would have hurt him. Moreover, he owed her money.

On the verge of tears, Claude turned round like Orpheus for Eurydice and met the grey-yellow eyes of the shadow which had swept through the revolving doors behind him. That look which clearly was not for him; Caroline Choukroun, as any good social animal nevertheless perceived its unusual effect. Worried that Claude wanted to talk to her, she hastily placed her hand on his arm with the soft dismissive gesture of a bodyguard, and pushed him away, walking towards the centre of the room, while turning automatically to her followers in order to avoid coming face-to-face. Her companion happened to be Medora. Claude understood what was happening, which added to his confusion. He felt like a lost child whose mother is no longer waiting for him, and who can be comforted by any woman, as long as she is kind.

The lights went out in the hall. The show was about to start. He hoisted himself onto a radiator to see the *runway*. At his feet like everywhere else in the aisles set up between the tiered rows of seats, the crowd *standing* were packed tight, blocked by security. His eyes fell again on the white mask of the woman he had once loved. This second apparition, less confusing, left him time for a detailed scrutiny. Jostled by the newcomers pushing their way in, and the security pushing back, N was trying to maintain her composure. Claude thought she looked provincial with her bag stuffed under her arm like a good middle-class woman, and the idea made him suffer even more, hurtful as it was to his self-esteem. Next to her, a small man with dyed black hair was trying to catch a glimpse of the show, probably the 'old Jew full of cash' whom he'd heard about from acquaintances. Claude closed his eyes.

To forget N, he searched in his memory for a beach other than the one in Palma, an ocean bay where he planned to drown himself. A choice that had been carefully considered: Etretat lacked austerity, he didn't know the North Sea well enough, and Brittany seemed to be reserved for middle-class holidays. In Biarritz the ocean was too wild and he didn't feel any attraction for the Landes. Only the Cotentin pleased him with its romanticism, especially the surroundings of the centre for recycling of atomic waste in La Hague. Like an employee thinks about his holiday he nourished the project, the journey to the Bay of Ecalgrain. Often in the night before falling asleep, filled with a solemn and serene emotion, he anticipated this last departure. No bags, the underground as far as the Saint-Lazare station, a second-class ticket for Cherbourg. He would climb into a compartment, sit under a black and white picture of a blossoming apple tree or a view of the Mont-Saint-Michel. He is lulled by the diesel of the turbo-train which takes him through the big Parisian wastelands of the Sernam towards the western forests, the basilica of Lisieux, little Theresa's hair, the plain of Caen and the marshes of Lassay…

He was busy with the funeral arrangements, and the sorrow of his friends when, opening his eyes to let a tear drop, he saw an apparition before him in the place where Niki had been standing a few moments earlier, the head of the sexagenarian junkie: Ira A. The same Ira he had met in former times at Ben Chemoul's, in Saint Tropez, then loved the year after in Paris. Ira A couldn't see him against the light, perched on his radiator, and anyway she wouldn't have recognized him. (He was used to it.) Past sixty, with a Gorgon's head and the eyes of a dead fish, she looked like an Egyptian portrait from the Fayoum. Claude remembered having seen her in a pornographic photo-story Ali had shown him. She appeared in the company of Napoleon, a bogus Napoleon, of course. Poor Ira A, rich in her Hollywood origins, her Roman filmography, her jet-set husbands and, now, changed into a weird oversized fairy.

The show was coming to an end, the designer appeared on the *runway* and Ali applauded. From a distance he saw Claude climbing down from his radiator, leaning on the shoulder of a second Claude, an old junkie who acted as companion to the former actress Ira A. Ali adored actresses and as he didn't know many, he was content with those who were at his level, gutter-level. Rushing towards the two Claudes and their lady friend, he passed Niki who didn't recognize him and whom he didn't recognize either. Ira A (or, as Ali screeched: Iraaa!!!) was talking to herself in her big cracked voice, typical of mature junkies. Claude 1 was looking gloomy as usual, while Claude 2 raised his chin to try to locate Anita, an old groupie of the Rolling Stones who had remarried a Rasta. True to form, Ali launched directly onto the opposite tack to impose himself on the trio.

"I always liked the Beatles best."

To which Claude 2 replied:

"Me, I've slept with a Beatle."

One wonders which one of the Beatles could have slept with Claude 2. Particularly as his brain, mushed by drugs, jumbled all the names of the bands. He could just as well have slept with a Beach Boy or even with a guy who resembled an old Beatle, or even just with someone bearded. Or, quite conceivably, he could have invented the whole thing. But as Claude 2 dressed as a woman at the beginning of the seventies, it was possible that an alcohol-fuelled Beatle, like Ringo Starr, had made a mistake. That day, Claude 2 was fifty-three. After having "a snifter" backstage, he wanted to "throw a little party". What he meant was: to What he meant was: to buy a gram or two of pink heroin from an Arab. The Franco-American actress, who didn't do anything without her sherpa, let herself float in his wake like a giant inert jelly-fish, her eyelids half-lowered over her sea-green eyes cast brief glances towards the black ceiling and mouldings in stucco of the old theatre which resembled, thought Claude, so many petrified spectators.

"My bum is itchy."

It was Ali calling everybody's attention to himself. From the collection of social catch-phrases Ali used to revive a conversation, the physiological mention of an intimate nature was his first resource.

"Stop, I'm getting hard."

In Claude 2, he had found the perfect partner. Not too fussy in the repartee department. Together they sounded right: two ageing poofs who, although bristling with many grounds for hostility (they couldn't stand each other, and that had been going on for thirty years already), both sacrificed themselves to the duties of their burden: the cult of pretty boys and scatological jokes.

The foursome went through the red curtain that marked the entrance to the backstage world. While Ali and Claude the homosexual disappeared in search of leftover, half-drunk champagne, Claude the melancholic stood to one side. As the backstage area filled, a motley crew of people whose disparate appearance was only a façade, crammed in together in front of his eyes. Fundamentally bound by the rhizomes of a common passion, they only found themselves in conflict with each other in the game of diverging interests or the chance of physical qualities, sometimes grotesque, sometimes angelic. Rare were the lost strays who were not captivated: disparate pieces in the entourage of 'the designer's family', country bumpkins, young girls abandoned by their booker.

Babsi and her like hadn't entirely disappeared from Claude's life. Since he had reduced his daily dose of anti-psychotics, they sometimes appeared at the edge of his perception. Helped by champagne, Claude caught a glimpse, at the back of the room, in the shadow of shadows, framed in the background between two of society's buffoons, of one of those little ghosts looking at him with the eye of a fairy. A ghost-glance, with which the real Babsi undoubtedly seduced the Turkish immigrants when she was selling her charms in 1976, baby-hustling at the Berlin Zoo Station. At that precise moment, Claude heard a high-pitched voice utter something like *"voodoo doll"*. It was probably nothing like that. Nothing voodoo-like in that mandrake, whose skin had the pale-blue freshness of a German dawn. Claude thought in his heart of hearts that a soft shampoo would make her hair more bouncy and bring back the sunny, *grünenwaldien* yellow which was its natural colour. That princess of the dawn, as beautiful as the rising of the sun over the Wansee, as fierce as the voices of Marshal Joukov's soldiers 'hey German girl, hey German girl', as sweet and secretive as the fruit of a gang rape, as charming as a fatherless child, was looking at Claude with eyes as blind as those of the portrait of the Little Dead Girl. And even if it didn't see him, that look for him was sweeter than the most fertilizing aperture offered by a living being: love of nature and of ghosts often go hand in hand.

The society buffoons in the foreground stepped aside and the shadow-theatre became more interesting: a cowboy and a Chinese transvestite surrounded the pseudo-Babsi, lavished with their self-seeking attentions. Like Anna May Wong in a Joseph von Sternberg drama, the transvestite, whom Claude identified as someone called Lychee (formerly Kim), and who was at the time hanging around in the entourage of the *coutu-rier* Claude Montana, was putting on the picturesque airs of an addicted *sous-maîtresse* in a French concession in Shanghai, and was smoking what should have been an Abdullah, but was undoubtedly nothing more than a Salem menthol, in si-lence, enigmatic to the point of caricature, her hand placed on the naked shoulder of the pseudo-Babsi (a fourteen-year-old Czechess who had landed the day before yesterday for *fashion week*). As for the man with the Stetson, a male body-builder straight out of an issue of *Pictorial Physique* from the fifties, he was moving his belly forward towards his prey, as he spoke, seeming—from Claude's point of view (but surely it was an optical illusion)—to rub the worn fly of his blue jeans against the thin membrane of skin which protected the still unsullied mouth of the girl, from Claude's point of view (but surely it was an optical illusion). Shepherded by those two, mused our hero, there was no way she would finish an old spinster, nor ignore for long the road to the chemist.

A shove made him lose sight of the trio. Ali next to him—Claude could feel the warmth of his shoulder against his—was having a conversation with an old effeminate adolescent with a protruding Adam's apple. When he was young, Claude had been so attractive to mortals that he had to protect himself from their approaches. Today though he was old and ugly, he'd kept that same slightly haughty stiffness which made him look pretentious. Pretention to tranquillity, rather modest pretention, but pretention nevertheless, in the eyes of the world, and thus in the eyes of the old boy from the past who was Ali's friend, and who was looking daggers at him. Consequently the empty eyes of the little apparition seemed even more charitable and more sweet.

But what was Claude really seeing? Modern psychiatry which had prescribed him his drugs, no longer even acknowledges that the patient has the gullibility needed for hallucinatory visions. Recent publications rule out the discourses of the mad concerning those apparitions of whom they pretend to be victim. According to the doctors, it would seem that even the craziest patients don't have a blind belief in the reality of the spirits which affect them. Or rather, they believe without believing, suspecting deep down, that the trees covered in blood, the talking birds, the little girls with the muddy hair and the eyes of a painting, belong to a category of reality inferior to their evening bowl of noodles or the Audi of their psychiatrist.

"Toto adores little bitches when they are frizzy."

Ira A, who had come back to life thanks to the champagne, had gathered her spirits well enough to be able to talk to Ali (or, actually, to a clothes rack laden with dresses and a full-length mirror, for Ali had turned away). She was tackling her favourite subject: the life of her dog Toto. A subject which didn't interest anyone (apart from perhaps Suzan, a Swiss-German former call-girl whose dog had health problems too, except Suzan was not there) but passionately interested Ira A to the point of giving her voice a vibrato taut with emotion. Reflected in the three-sided mirror, Ali's head was shiny with sweat and his scars, courtesy of a failed hair-implant, showed a kind of pinkish ring like a monk's tonsure. Furious that Ali was so little interested in her Toto, Ira A stretched her hand towards the bald head.

"It's disgusting that thing you have on your head, it looks like a dilated anus."

And she laughed in the same way others cough.

Ali, busy maneuvering in an uncertain seductive attempt on the 'curly-haired twink' who guarded the ice box, felt quite humiliated. But—and he was not making a habit of it—he did not know what to reply.

"Ira, my love, we're going, we have some shopping to do."

Always ready for the call of drugs, the former star of Cinecitta quivered like a vampire invited to a ball, and abandoned her victim, abruptly turning her back on him. Dead to all sense of shame, Ali jumped on Claude 2 and asked him if he 'had anything'.

"No, but come with us, I have my mother's Renault 5, we're going shopping, you have some cash?"

"Of course," the Arab confirmed. "Claude, are you coming, we're going to do drugs."

Claude understood, by Ali's generosity, that he must have visited the handbags in the cloakroom.

"Ooh, I see, still very dubious, you fags."

It was little Marc, an expert in the field.

"Are you coming, Marco? After, we can go to Porte Dauphine to celebrate my birthday, if you want."

"Out of the question, I'm finished with wogs. Have a new fiancé, a bisexual swimming-instructor. I'm faithful. Stop laughing Ali or I shit on your head."

"People say you have Aids?"

"You're getting on my nerves, all of you. I don't have Aids, I had cancer, that's why I lost weight."

"Farida told me you were ill."

"That cunt of an Arab, she'd better take care of her crabs."

"Farida has crabs?"

"Yes, and d'you know who told me? Prepare yourself for a shock: Mouna Ayoub."

"Sorry!"

It was the man with the cowboy hat, accompanied by the young girl and the transvestite, who wanted to squeeze past Marc.

"Eh, mate, isn't she a bit young? You're not going to stretch her I hope. Not that I care, personally I don't like children. I only like big dicks."

"You two look like each other, two brothers I'd say."

"Thanks a lot, Ira, it's kind of you to compare me to that horror. I'll give it back to you."

Marc had spoken a bit too loudly, as usual. At the word 'horror', the man with a stetson turned round. The *roadies* were dismantling the spotlights, and a searchlight fleetingly lit up what was under the hat. As if seeing a demon, Claude Boudin collapsed behind Ali who was at least four inches shorter than him.

"Come to my place one of these days, baby. I'll do you good."

With a very disturbing kindness, the cowboy had softly let drop that answer meant for Marc.

"Oh yeah, you want to show me your big dick?"

The other guy stayed silent for a moment, to enforce his inevitable response. Opposite him, the group had closed ranks under the threat, suddenly standing together like old animals surprised to see that they can still be led to the slaughterhouse. There was no more nastiness, not the shadow of perversity, not a single cynic in action, only old timid sheep that would have preferred that the butcher's knife was for their neighbour rather than for themselves. They had even started to smell a bit, like those rodents whose glands give off evil smells to disgust their predators.

"No, I'll give you a little massage. There's nothing better to revive the senses."

The little Czechess tried to free herself, but the man only had to squeeze her arm tight for her to return to his side.

"If you see your friend, the one who left to hide in the john, could you tell him his sister sends her kisses … "

Ali turned to Claude, who had indeed disappeared.

Meanwhile in the toilets, a photographer in search of images for a music video he was making on a 'low budget'— according to the producer's instructions—without much idea himself about the storyboard (the musicians, without much talent or enthusiasm, didn't 'feel' any of the 'concepts' proposed to them) was marvelling at a spectacle he found absolutely fascinating: the urinals of the Elysée-Montmartre filled with ice-cubes dumped by the waiters after the cocktail was over. He was pointing out this 'completely metaphysical' image of the white receptacles filled with translucent balls on which blue disinfectant flowed like a topping of Obao to his female assistant (a kind of salsify with blond hair).

Facing the vegetable-like response of the salsify, the young artist reinforced his opinion with an idiomatic expression he used and abused tirelessly:

"It's genius," he said, inspired. "Take a Polaroid."

While the salsify was extracting the Polaroid camera from a neat satchel on which the word *'Fuck'* was written, an unexpected apparition came to help, in his way, the construction of the shot the photographer was already framing in space with his fingers joined together in a square. A very pale old man who could have made a credible walk-on part in *The Night of the Living Dead*, appeared from nowhere. His reflection, reproduced *ad infinitum* in the mirrors above the basins, gave the impression of an army of staggering ghosts charging a world deserted by the living. The old man gone, the photographer picked up some medication from the floor.

"Look, he dropped this. Do you think it's good stuff?"

The photographer took off his tinted glasses to read the instructions he had extracted from the green and white box.

"Genius! It's an 'anti-psychotic' to use if you hear voices when there's nobody there, or when you see things that don't exist. It must give you hallucinations."

"Do you think it's fattening?" asked the salsify.

Ira A and her faithful knights found themselves on a pavement shining in the warm night, an inverted sky in which the lights from the Turkish sandwich-sellers were reflected like the canopy of heaven on a miniature Bosphorus. Ira and Claude 2 crossed the boulevard arm-in-arm manoeuvring between the cars. Claude, still very dishevelled despite his Zyprexa, hung on in his friend Ali's wake. As for Marc, he had stayed there, standing before the Elysée-Montmartre, to stare at the young Arabs passing along the boulevard, smacking his fleshy lips like a prowling cabaret tout. Except for the fact that the only spectacle he had for sale was himself. Ali wondered aloud what age Claude 2's mum was to still own that neat little Renault 5. At least ninety, he imagined for he remembered that twenty years earlier, Ira had told him that this star of styling had parents who were already old.

"Hey, guys, wait for me! You'll never guess with whom I last climbed into a Renault 5." Marc hadn't endured solitude for long. "Hold on to your hats, it was with Nabila Khashoggi."

"Again! Are you two sleeping together?"

"No, not Mouna Ayoub, cunt, Nabila Khashoggi. We were in Marbella, at her father's, who was in prison in Switzerland. And the villa staff, fifty altogether, were on strike because they hadn't been paid for six months. They had even confiscated the keys of the limousine. So we borrowed the gardener's Renault 5 to go and buy some food. There wasn't even a biscuit left in the kitchen. Hey, no, Ira, you're too fat plus you smell of pee. I prefer to ride in the boot. Throw me out at the Porte de la Chapelle, will you?"

Ira spat out a few homophobic insults destined for the abuser.

"That's it, that's it, take your pills, old cunt. I'd rather hitch-hike with Arabs, at least they have big dicks and some crack."

Marc left, sticking out his thumb into the beam of headlights. The poor wandering soul who, at eighteen, had been (of which the passers-by were completely unaware) the radiant lover of Luchino Visconti, crossed by without seeing, on the embankment beside the boulevard Rochechouaurt, another soul in pain whom the girls of the night, guardians of the natural order, had already abandoned. Accompanied by the cowboy, the young girl and an old lady in red leatherette trousers who remained anonymous, Lychee, the self-styled 'queen of the Bois de Boulogne' passed by, her heavy aura brushing lightly against Claude, whom she thought was the most 'fuckable' passenger in the Renault 5. She asked him for a light, with the same pout as Lauren Bacall in *Key Largo*. Leaning towards the proffered lighter, she caressed Claude with her dark eyes filled with promises.

"Never fall for boys with brown hair, Lychee, it's bad luck."

Her chaperone—the one in leatherette—returned her verdict and the little group disappeared into the cowboy's Ford Mustang. Claude exchanged glances with the 'queen of the Bois de Boulogne' not knowing that it would be for the last time. A few weeks later, Lychee would be nothing more than a cadaver in a forest.

"Che-mist-o-pen-night-and-day-From-to-mor-row-I-must-love-my-self-Al-co-hol-a-buse-is-a-health-haz-ard."

Barely floating across the surface of the surrounding noises, Ira A's voice chanted a kind of rabbinical prayer. Claude understood that the former interpreter of Mauro Bolognini was struck by that awful habit peculiar to children and certain elderly persons, which involved, as soon as they were seated in a car, reading every signboard and advertising poster in a high voice, pronouncing every syllable.

It was a lovely evening. They went first to Strasbourg-Saint-Denis to buy that cheap heroin called *brown sugar* that Claude 2 pretended to prefer to superior quality drugs. "I had the best *brown* in Paris for three hundred francs a gram at the Wimpy in Place Clichy," he flung at his passengers, from his fifty-three years as a purist. After having snorted half of the package in front of the others, Ali suffered the first indisposition, symptomatic of that kind of intoxication: he vomited *chewarma*, Gini and champagne not necessarily in that order through the window of the Renault 5. The incident obviously annoyed the driver (the interior door fittings were completely covered) and upset the passengers, except for Ira who 'couldn't smell anything since her hemiplegia'. Disgusted by the idea of accompanying them to the Bois de Boulogne, the partner of Edwige Fenech in *Four Willies Salute You* demanded, in a very lady-like way, to be dropped off at the Champ-de-Mars then, once re-assured, giving in to the emotion which was one of the psychotropic effects of heroin, she started on an evocation of her dog Toto's tricks, which provoked in Ali, just barely restored, another undesirable consequence of heroin, the light drowsiness that junkies call in drug-speak: 'to nod off'.

Having reached the Champ-de-Mars, Claude 2 was surprised to see his protegée walking towards a certain ground-floor apartment.

"Darling, are you sure you're still living at Sao Schlumberger's place?"

Ira suddenly remembered that she didn't reside at Mme Sao Schlumberger's, who hadn't talked to her for fifteen years, but the rue d'Alger, at Felix N'Goudou's, a new acquaintance. That return to the right bank was only the first of our friends' wanderings, which led them to the Bois de Boulogne, or, more precisely, to an avenue situated in the vicinity of the Russian

Embassy, nicknamed, because of what happened there, wanker's alley, then to a bar in rue de Ponthieu, and finally to a special establishment in the Opera neighbourhood where Claude 2, whose birthday was being celebrated that evening, as the attentive reader will have remembered, succeeded, thanks to that argument (that it was his birthday) and with some difficulty, in convincing the night watch-man of a Maghrebi supermarket to do him a favour in the form of brief anal intercourse. The intercourse took place at rue Rosa-Bonheur, in the bedroom that Claude 2 had as a child, next to the room where his mum (aged eighty-nine) slept the restless sleep of the elderly. As for Ali, he had fallen into the peaceful slumber of drug addicts in the backroom of that special establishment near the Opera. Claude 1 had walked home by himself, trying to count how many evenings similar to this one he had spent since 1976. He reached the number 4,500. As for his fellow companions in fortune, of whatever sex, their number must have reached around 10,000.

The vehicles which conveyed them, and which had ranged from a moped to a Rolls Royce, with, in between, all sorts of vans, three-wheelers, company cars, shooting-brakes, electric mini-cars, sometimes with a driver, sometimes without heating, often driven in a masterly manner by alcoholics, at times stopped by the forces of law and order, once flanked by a police escort, that ill-assorted ensemble represented the number of private cars of a provincial sub-prefecture like Pithiviers. Claude had had seventeen road accidents, two of which were serious; he had taken part or witnessed a high number of disputes, people fainting, rows; ingested heaps of variously toxic substances, drunk casks of wine and spirits. He had experienced the same nights in Paris, London, Madrid, Rome, Milan and even once in New York, not to mention the summer resorts and the ski resorts ... He had been at discotheques in La Beauce, in Poitou, in the back of beyond and he had even sat down in the only gay bar in Aurillac. The subjects of the conversations during those moments were as diverse as those of a Renaissance book, and to give an index would be impossible. Instead let's imagine a conversation at table that lasted 6,000 nights, in which one could find, in quantity, dealt with in a mostly superficial fashion—but at times with the most peculiar ideas, due to the nocturnal character of these talks, the rambling imposed by circumstances, the intemperance of the talkers and some eccentricities of which no one is exempt—matters of wide-ranging material allied with more modest preoccupations or practical advice.

Obviously, the mass of spheres tackled didn't represent the universal and the use of statistics (Plato the philosopher twice quoted in twenty-two years against more than 100,000 occurrences of several synonyms for the verb 'to copulate') would have revealed the main subjects of interest and lack of interest of that sub-group of the middle-class which had had access, during the final decades of the twentieth century, to a mode of nocturnal pleasures reserved in the past for the richest: the *dolce vita.* Not much had remained of those words, obviously. Amongst these activities, rare were those which had benefited Claude. But the repetition, the chain of events, represented not only an ensemble of information in which he could search (recipe for sauté shrimps from a Laotian transvestite, viewpoint on eternal life from an Italian press attaché, imaginary confidences on the sexual life of Catherine Deneuve from people in the know), but also a solid mass which gave him the feeling of a rich thickness on which his social legitimacy was based, as well as the elitist morality which followed from it. Vanity allowed him to estimate highly the value of his own experience, even if the so-called experience was only that of carelessness, neglect, lack of money and disgust. The worst being that elitism is a feeling as common as it is impossible to share, and this experience collided daily with other experiences slightly inferior or superior (never an equality in the elite), which led him to grotesque conversations and wounded pride.

Now for example, to be honest, Claude didn't feel any particular embarrassment concerning the mediocre way he had spent his evening. He was actually rather proud to have spent it with a film star, never mind that Ira A had only talked to him once, to him Claude Boudin—a former lover—to ask him to wind up the car window of the Renault for her neck was getting slightly cold. The state of the lady only added to his retrospective pleasure. Like those connoisseurs of scrap metal markets who appreciate even more a saucepan or an old mottled stove if they lack handles or if they look as if they've been left in the mud for years, Claude and his friends as we've said earlier, particularly worshipped the idols fallen to their level, especially if they were of the weaker sex. Which is incidentally a bad habit shared by many gay men.

In that happy frame of mind, Claude went up the boulevard Magenta, allowing his memory to make a list of the circumstances which had led him to meet famous people, while looking forward to being back in his dear house, and to enjoy some good reading under his dear street lamp. At this moment: *Les Petites Filles modèles* by the Comtesse de Ségur, and *The Decline of the West* by Oswald Spengler.

Finding the apartment in the same state as it was when they had left gave Claude the blues. Automatically he started to put away his old papers in the darkness. He came across a large photo, a black and white shot of Niki and Marina, posing at a party, each with a glass of wine and a cigarette. The photographer had dedicated it: 'For Claude, affectionately, my two passions. François.' He was alluding to the wine and cigarettes, not the two models.

In the grasp of a drunk's sudden impulse, Claude uttered a pathetic shriek and grabbed a strip of capsules he mistook in the dark for his Zyprexa. He swallowed them all with a glass of tap water. Thinking he was about to die, he lay down on his mattress, the photo rolled up in his hand.

The next day he awoke looking really superb: in error he had swallowed one of those self-tanning strips Ali left lying around everywhere.

"I am very sorry to have to tell you that 'the Wolf-Man' does not feel up to making any new friends or acquaintances, and has asked me not to give his address to anyone. He is now eighty-five years of age, and very frail."

WHEN CLAUDE VISITED the ground floor of the avenue Georges-Mandel, where he had known so many adventures, nothing of the past remained. The big photographic portraits of made-up children, the Napoleon III poufs with their pompons, which had sat unnaturally beside plastic garden chairs, the soiled carpets and soft sofas especially adapted for the education of vice, had disappeared. Only the old french windows, jammed half open, and the roses in the garden remained, witnesses to the bacchanals of 1976. The apartment had been sold and the new owners were going to spend between '700 and 900,000 bucks' on the works, according to little Philippe. Little Philippe was a former acquaintance of Ben Chemoul's, who now worked in real estate. He still had the steel watch 'the master' had given him and the keys to the apartment whose sale he had organized. Ben Chemoul's *chinese eyes* Rolls Royce was no longer in the garage though a large oil stain covered with a soaked piece of cardboard was still there. At the back, in the darkness, there was a pile of books: works by Gérard de Villiers, a manual for cigar smokers and an English psychology book from which Claude had just read that quotation.

At the time when Claude and Marina visited him the doctor was in his fifties, bearded and and obese, and when not in consultation spent most of his time in his underpants, dancing to 45s, drinking tea and talking on the phone with mysterious correspondents. His favourite record was *Bang Bang* by Sheila, to which he danced the *paso doble*, hugging a pillow to make the children laugh. As little Sophie used to say, he was a character.

Nowadays, when some educationalists are severely criticized, it can still seem scandalous to talk about such a case. But 'the Ben Chemoul method' was quite a success. The children liked him, for he was funny, even if they used to call him 'the gorilla' because of the hair covering his back; funnier than ordinary psychiatrists; funnier than their parents too. One had fun in the avenue Georges-Mandel. There were masked balls, tombolas, surprises, dangerous games and the Rolls Royce. One was scared too, but, as little Sophie used to say, 'the best times are when one is scared'. The whole of Ben Chemoul's educational project was contained in that sentence written by a friend of his, a French writer he was always quoting: *As for me, I have chosen, I shall be on the side of crime and I shall help the children, not to go back to your houses, your factories, your schools, your laws and sacraments, but to violate them.* He used to call family life a monstrous limitation of affectivity. According to him, there was nothing surprising in the fact that a child looked elsewhere for what he or she needed. His theory justified sexual crimes by putting forward the victim's secret desire to be a victim. For example, he read in Marina's lightness (she used to weigh less than thirty-five kilos) the manifestation of her desire to be lifted from the ground by a ravisher and, to suit the action to the word, he used to lift her to the ceiling, laughing like an ogre. The head of the child, half-terrorised, half-laughing, made the crystals of the chandelier tinkle. For him, the parental couple was nothing but an unbearable unit and the place for all fake feelings: a mother could as well not want to breast feed or to love, a father to get rid of his children, and both wish to be rid of each other. Against family and its ideology, he praised the role of the protector. In order to protect his little flock and to allow his sheep to scatter across the big wide world (for example through prostitution which he called the true free love and judged preferable to any work—especially with the family until the grave), he lied to parents and posed as an ordinary psychiatrist, defender of social order and middle-class morality.

Contrary to most of the regulars of avenue Georges-Mandel who had come to terms with the 'gorilla's blah-blah' (they saw him as a kind of distributor of fifty franc notes, to be avoided after five in the morning), Marina felt confused by these theories which devalued her own feelings: everything rested on a hypothetical desire she'd never really felt—and, on top of that, she liked her brother and her parents. Not to disappoint people with whom she was pleased to be (Ben Chemoul of course, but also those girlfriends from her set and others she met at night), she convinced herself that she was wrong and did her best to avoid conflicts by submitting to the common law. It wasn't long before she lost interest in everything that was to do with physical love and with her own body in particular. Sometimes she no longer felt her body at all, a bit like the time the ear, nose and throat specialist from the rue Saint-Simon had given her anaesthetics with a mask when they removed her adenoids. At other times she felt like she was seeing herself act, as if she was outside herself. It looked like a movie on television. And if she gave herself, it was not like Eva or Pauline, for the benefits she could extract (even if her heroin addiction was starting to bother her too), but because she didn't see any valid reason to refuse. Never mind the integrity of her body, never mind the rubbing of her soft skin against less fragile materials, never mind all the things they wanted to do to her, as an object she gave herself to rites that didn't concern her. Above all, she felt that she was loved precisely for that: her intimate docility contradicted her provocative look. However, if she was docile as far as her body was concerned, she showed much more energy in defending Claude. Which was not always useful for the latter, though as insensitive to physical love as his little sister, he was more easily scared of getting hurt.

If the body was nothing for them, the clothes, the hairstyles they wore represented the essential. At the time, this group of children shared a taste for being admired. Their whole attitude tended to that. As a result, they didn't forgive each other the slightest mistakes, the tiniest neglect. They were getting ready, doing each other's hair, inspecting each other like an elite division before battle. If some slept there, most didn't arrive at avenue Georges-Mandel before the middle of the afternoon. Around five, there was deafening chaos in front of the tailor's three-sided-mirror.

The mirror had been removed with the rest of the furniture but Claude found its old spot in one of the little salons, a semi-circular room whose three French windows (locked now with shutters), had in the past coloured with an incomparable golden glaze, the triple-perspective-mirror around which the fauns and young nymphs had crammed, which multiplied the planes in that tight space, as in the painting by Correggio which decorated Ben Chemoul's bedroom. That light from the past still reached Claude despite all the doors that age had closed at the end of the corridor of time, beyond the darkness of the bleak years which had followed, that light—of spring, of course—of an evening in June—the magnificent western light, when the sun was about to plunge beyond the Bois de Boulogne, the race tracks, the hills of Saint-Cloud, casting onto the green velvet of the big park rays brighter than the scale of colour that the sun drew on the naked wall. The sun of today filtered through the slats of the blinds. That light was also one of childhood, or rather that extreme childhood when shared experiences, the confidences of yesterday's parties, the laughter and screams, but also the lack of physical differentiation, the confusing re-semblances, the close-as-twin relationships made what was about to happen unthinkable: the parting of the group into individual destinies, the burying of the social, worldly, commu-nal, unselfish being into the solitary tomb of adulthood.

On some days, the girls used to come back from the flea market with bags of second-hand clothes that they tried on, screaming like sirens. Priceless treasures, like that pair of five-inch high stilettos in black cobra-skin patent size three, were snatched, passed from hand to hand until a lucky Cinderella (on that day, little Mado) received from her fellows with longer toes, absolute rights to them, not without having to give up something 'valuable' 'at once' in exchange to little Pierre, who had 'nicked' them from a boutique in Place Sainte-Opportune. The bathroom at the end of the corridor, where nobody ever washed, was a slightly quieter gathering spot. In the stench of tobacco and cheap hairspray, one could glimpse, through the narrow opening of the door, behind an anonymous mingling of naked golden legs resting on the basin, some tiny Venus at the mirror touching the corner of her eyelid with her chubby fingers to adjust some fake eyelashes.

In theory, around nine o'clock, all of them were impeccable. At the beginning especially, for later, through visiting nightclubs regularly, they had found steady admirers and therefore, the routine changed. They had felt the need to be together diminishing all the time. They could even allow themselves some deviations, some 'moments without', some small infidelities they would have thought impossible five months earlier. At the beginning they were very serious, very smart, very punctual. But their psychological flaws, their instabilities, were betrayed by mood swings, violence, blows; the fits of hysterics were frequent and the presence of several epileptics made matters worse. After a crisis, they had to start all over again, re-sew, re-crimp, redo the make-up. That took time and it wasn't unusual that at ten o'clock, when Ben Chemoul was calling the troops together, there were always two or three who were not ready.

Ben Chemoul, who would have happily stayed in his underpants if it had been possible, was wearing for the occasion a more formal suit, always perfectly white, which was a challenge for his Filipino servant, for he ate often, and messily. Most concerned about his appearance, the doctor had found in this white uniform a personal style which made his voluminous silhouette immediately recognizable. When he stepped out of his dressing room, twirling like a young ballerina, or rather like one of those bears that gypsy-tamers dress up as brides to amuse their audience, he was waiting for the applause. But the children, who 'knew his act by heart' didn't show any particular enthusiasm, except if they intended to be up for a fifty franc note, or a place in the Rolls.

"Maurice, you're superb!"

Little Eva needed to be seriously in withdrawal to show such enthusiasm which, although relative—she had pronounced those words with the intonation of a sleep-walker consenting to a séance of hypnosis—clashed with the girl's usually sullen character. At any compliment which made him happy, the 'gorilla' stopped in front of the adjustable mirror, whose three sides he easily filled, and, sinking into an ecstatic contemplation of himself, stroked his beard and slightly adjusted the dent of his borsalino, whose ribbon alone would have been sufficient to dress that young drug addict who, eager for her reward, reflected in the mirrors a triple little skull with anxious eyes.

"There, my Eva, since you're so kind today, have a Bounty."

In their jargon, a Bounty was a fifty franc note.

We are quite aware that such a trade between an adult and children placed in his care can appear indecent to the reader. It is not easy to reproduce the disturbing tinge of irony and apparent thoughtfulness which made the aberrations of the time acceptable. In those children, who were at different levels of mental instability before arriving at avenue Georges-Mandel, the doctor, by treating them with good nature, being their accomplice through laughter, through confidences concerning his own weaknesses, little rituals, a common jargon, and other artifices, had been able to develop morbid features which, alas, were only waiting to be confirmed. Nothing is more contagious than cynicism when it resembles sincerity. By laughing about everything, refusing to take offence at anything, systematically turning the good into bad—in Ben Chemoul's mouth, purity became stupidity, kindness became weakness and generosity turned into cowardice—and bad into good—laziness was in reality realism, cruelty was courage, and violence showed strength—that curious pedagogue had hardened their hearts and opened their minds to the most immoral of perspectives. And everybody knows that childhood offers itself to crime with a fearless joy.

"Do you know what has become of Eva?"

"That cunt? She overdosed."

Claude looked at little Philippe who had just pronounced that funeral oration with classic sobriety in the hard tone of their set from the past.

If between themselves they showed little disposition to compassion, vis-à-vis the outside world, it was worse.

At the beginning, it looked like they didn't want to seduce at all. Especially the girls, who generally were disagreeable with the people who approached them, and were only interested in their little gang. Then, things had begun to change, and as they were becoming more civilized—for example, by talking or making love with more people—they had lost their haughtiness and, at the same time, most of their mysterious grace in the eyes of those who desired them. So inevitably they had become more obliging, more anxious too, they were measuring their effect against their first success, trying to cash in with their antics. They were like little girls who have been paid a compliment for an apt or touching expression and who try to generate new praise by pulling faces. Only a few amongst the most extreme, like little Sophie, took refuge in an aggressivity that her drug addiction made invulnerable. From her fourteenth year, despite a permanent near-nudity which threw her at the mercy of the worst company, Sophie reacted savagely and never hesitated to use violence: spitting, fists, hand weapons, not to protect herself for she was easily physically approached, and by anybody, but to discourage all attempts to tame her or control her outbursts. At the same time greedy, stealing, a 'trouble maker', and totally disinterested, she never missed an opportunity to behave badly, so much so that she was 'barred' from several nightclubs. Even Ben Chemoul got bored with her torrent of abuse and the permanent upsets of which she was the cause. If he kept her in his little gang, it was solely for her beauty. Sophie jumped from a window in an apartment in Trastevere in Rome at the end of the seventies. The story went that her fierce temperament hadn't withstood time either, the young beauty was living at the end of her life with a lesbian photographer who had succeeded, it seemed, in softening her a little.

The flock was trying by means fair or foul to find grounds for, if not satisfaction, at least hope in the management of the adults who succeeded in thwarting them. A thousand small perversities, a taste for profligate stealing, venereal diseases, a lack of personal hygiene, not to mention bulimia, drug addiction, alcoholism and twilight states, in no time made the company of these children too hard to bear for the very people abusing them. Consequently the 'punters' didn't last long, and after a few days of absence, the young person came back, empty-handed, after having left triumphantly with the highest hopes of making a record or going for a screen-test. In the gang's jargon, that kind of misadventure was called 'a trip to Japan', referring to little Edwigette's bragging, in the past, when she had claimed she was accompanying a famous singer on his Japanese tour, before returning the next day on the first metro, her throat covered in bruises.

"Camille, it's great, I met a fat Jew, full of money, who's taking me to Gstaad."

"Yeah, right, Madeleine, have a nice trip to Japan. See you tomorrow."

"You cunt!"

In the same basements, next to the punters, there were sometimes people whose attention the little ones desperately wanted to attract, and who had gained entrance, no-one knew exactly how. These last minute guests often belonged to the record or film industry, but not always. Generally they were ex-prostitutes who had done well, one by making love with Visconti, another by marrying a Rolling Stone. Ex-bellboy, ex-call-girl, they had managed to come out of their impecunious adolescence, making use of their bodies, their kisses, without working and succeeding with one opportune fuck. Today they were doing little else but drugs, partying or flirting with younger people. They were famous without being entitled to it. And if, sometimes, a talent re-awakened by chance, gave them an unexpected legitimacy, unlike professional artists, they didn't make a meal of it and never held boring conversations about their job. They were satisfied with seducing easy prey. For the little ones, these characters were semi-gods, for they resembled them a bit, though much better. When one starts in life, one needs role-models to help one to progress, and whose success gives one courage. One says to oneself: before, they used to be like us and now they are there, without having done a thing, strutting about and drinking champagne. They rent suites at the Plaza Athénée, they are truly free and don't have to touch Ben Chemoul for fifty franc notes. Ah, if only they could choose us for friends and help us to live like them. Of course, it was completely illusory for such people had never helped anybody except perhaps a gigolo to find some heroin on the way to their bed. And they didn't have any friends either, nor a lot of money (in fact, they had to rely on their benefactors). But like those poisoners who have the habit of trying their drugs on small animals, they were delighted to test their power on young prey, to have some fun by impressing them. The worst was that they communicated through simple contact the charm in which they were bathed, to all those who had the privilege to approach them. Knowing them, one felt better, more seductive though even more incapable of working or living normally. Their girlfriends, and even the punters, could smell that they had reached another level. The same for the nightclub managers: one could gain free entrance and have free drinks for at least a week. Those highly infected characters contaminated you with their brilliance like one of those mutant viruses: flu or legionnaire's disease, which arrived in Europe on the same flights of Pan Am or Concorde. Spend just one night with them and one was fucked, one didn't come back to earth that easily. Marina, for example, had grown 'an incredibly big head' (according to the others) at thirteen, when one evening Bianca Jagger had given her a single kiss on the mouth.

Today, a kiss from Bianca Jagger probably doesn't appeal to many. But at the time, in 1976, the reader can't imagine what it was worth. To see Bianca Jagger sitting there among the others, under the multi-coloured neon signs of Le 7's ceiling, was already a miracle. It had the same effect as Lourdes, or La Sallette, for the little shepherds who had seen the Virgin. She had given her a kiss just like that, for a laugh, to amuse Helmut Berger's double (or perhaps it was the real one, Claude never knew) who was seated next to her. Because Marina was looking at her as if she was an apparition, and seeing that made-up little girl staring at her must have amused her. Anyway, she had seized her by the neck, approached her goddess lips and kissed her. That evening, Marina left the real world. She had begun to float, and so had Claude. He remembered that after the kiss, they were at the bar, all confused, and that he had seen in his sister's eyes something unknown. Even for him who knew her so well, she had become something else, something more mysterious, something more respectable. She had even started to look like the one who had kissed her. A smaller version of.

One shouldn't believe that people like Bianca Jagger don't realize the effect they produce. They had, it's true, given everything, betrayed everything, suffered everything for that effect. They were living off the admiration of the weakest like a vampire lives off the blood of virgins, and when one was bitten by them, one became like them, one had the imperious need to impress, to overwhelm children, to fascinate little girls. So when one didn't have the same means, one had to find one's audience elsewhere.

Claude remembered the saddest time with his sister in the winter of 1980, when they were trying to get some rest in a weekend cottage lent to them in Normandy, in the Vexin. It was cold, they heated the place with an oil-stove which filled the room with fumes, and they nourished themselves on Chamonix Orange and Laughing Cow. To pass the time, Claude did Marina's hair, no longer an enormous beehive but sleek locks like Veronica Lake. And as they didn't know what to do, on Sundays they used to leave the baby crying at home and go to the village mass. They went, sure of their effect, like two ghosts, to mesmerize little village girls who couldn't help but turn from the altar to look at Marina. Fairies or monsters, nevermind how they were seen, it made them feel good. Fascination, like fresh blood, gave them back their heart. They stole the show, not from Jesus, but from the priest. Better than nothing.

As for Ben Chemoul, he hated to have his glory stolen and that evening he hadn't stopped uttering sarcasms when referring to Marina and Bianca Jagger's kiss. While the little one, her cheek resting on the leather of the bench, smoked a Dunhill Menthol International, day-dreaming in the caress of dawn, he mocked her princess-like airs.

"You believe in yourself because you've kissed that old whore? It's disgusting to see."

Marina yawned without answering. Claude felt better than ever. Much more at home in the Rolls Royce than at school or at his parents'. This was life at its best.

PHOTOGRAPHED AS HE LEFT the Jumbo, a new club in rue Allard, in Saint-Tropez, Ira A's faithful admirer was a man with a curly head and beard who looked like the singer Herbert Pagani.

"Not bad," Ben Chemoul said, leaning over the shoulder of little Sylvie, as she cut French beans on the *Var-Nice-Matin* newspaper. The child-psychiatrist, usually not inclined to appreciate men younger than himself, was fraternally tolerant toward bearded men.

"Drop it, dad, it's an old paper I found in the cupboard."

Saying that, the young girl turned away to avoid the old man's soft beard which was disagreeably tickling her shoulder. Indifferent to the disgust he inspired, Ben Chemoul squeezed her even tighter, and, for no apparent reason, put his lips close to her ear, soft and downy like a puppy's tummy.

"Get off, dad, you stink of wine."

Ben Chemoul, not offended in the least, went back to his business.

In Claude's memory, that scene happened at the beginning of the splendid summer of 1976, which had been that of Marina's fourteenth birthday. She and Claude had only spent a few days together before she was invited by some people to go to Cannes. He had then been closer to Sylvie.

When the shadows lengthened, Claude and Sylvie used to hang about together in the hills. The moped jumped about on the dirt track and Sylvie often lost the espadrilles she was wearing as slippers. Claude had to put on the brakes so the girl could go hopping along, looking for the dusty shoes which were part, like the slipper of a black Virgin, of her delightful being. The delay, the manners of a hopscotch player annoyed Claude, who brushed her off. She jumped up again onto the back double-quick and tightened her warm hands, rough with dust, around the stomach of her faithful admirer. Sylvie was an English-speaking black girl who had landed, God knows how, in the little circle of the avenue Georges-Mandel. She unsettled our expectations of her race thanks to rather rare qualities: she didn't say anything and she had a long nose. A negress-fancier who made dubious deals with Ben Chemoul thought she resembled the statuette of a tribe whose name Claude had forgotten. It was Sylvie who had inspired our hero to write that famous couplet:

I like young girls
They are so sweet

Claude appreciated the moments spent with little Sylvie, all the more so for he felt lonely and her company, warm and fragrant (she was nubile and smelt of sweat) gave him the same reassuring feeling as the belly of the dog gives to one who sleeps on the street.

They used to go to a hill between Salins and Capon, near a house with green shutters which was closed up. They stretched on the terrace shaded by a maritime pine, on the bare cement, warm and cracked, and, most of the time, remained silent. Sylvie cracked open pine-nuts with a stone, and Claude, his head resting on her, could smell her flesh mingling with the scent of pine, wild plants and the warm motor of the moped parked nearby.

Some people are soothing and draw from those who accompany them, as if by magic, the sense of time passing, the dread of tomorrow, and, more generally, all worries linked to the future. The effect they have on us (we feel 'good' near them) comes from their personality, often nonchalant and, more mysteriously, from the physical sensation their bodies communicate to ours. There are beings with whom it's pleasant to hang around, who don't push at either working or dreaming. They are dangerous for spirits fond of activity. Claude risked nothing. Sometimes prostitutes have that disarming quality which has something in common with opium, but also with the charms sorceresses use in legends. The moderns see in it the effect of eroticism, but to have experienced once such a presence is enough to stop one making that mistake. The sexual attraction seems rather weak compared to such a medicine to which the water of Léthé alone—if it is one day given to us to drink—could be compared. The progressive reader will protest against the commonplace but negresses often trade in that type of charm.

When they came back in the night, and the headlight of the moped finally lit up the procession of oleanders which bordered the drive to the farm, they were starving. Usually Ben Chemoul had prepared the evening meal, with that delicate and never ponderous attention he applied to everyday tasks. From the various places he had lived, he had brought back some specific 'effects' which, put into practice, allowed him to vary his few recipes of Provençal or French-Algerian origin. His long stay in Cefalù, in Sicily, at the house of his master, Aleister Crowley, had especially helped him to simplify his culinary styles under the influence of Sicilian fishermen. That peasant sobriety gave his cooking an incomparable frankness and solidity.

Around the long wooden table on which hurricane lamps and bunches of wild flowers were lined, the guests, whose number changed depending on the moment, were seated. When they were small gatherings, Ben Chemoul used to choose one or two children to read. Claude, who read well, was often on duty. He had to choose from among the old paperbacks which smelt damp, and rekindle with his breath this or that dormant presence which fell from the book, along with a lost postcard or a pressed flower. Unlike those relics which turn to dust beneath the feet of the living, the apparitions aroused by his voice sprung up in the trembling light of the lamps, without interfering in the least with the ballet of the moths and nocturnal insects. One evening in July 1976, it was Mary, Queen of Scots who came into their midst as the remains of a fried chicken *à l'oranaise* were consumed. The beheading of the Rose of Scotland with an axe was exactly to the young man's taste, though he had come across it by chance. Hearing about the little white dog, covered in royal blood, which, appeared from beneath the scaffold and tried in vain to prevent the executioner's assistants from bearing away his mistress' remains, Suzy, a 'Madame' as one said at the time, who had just shown proof that she had a strong stomach by boasting about how she had sold her fifteen-year-old son to an Englishman, ordered Claude to stop because it was 'too sad'. The ex-owner of a hotel in Megève, who looked like a famous lawyer from Marseilles (blow-dried hair on a boozer's head, small pinky eyes) took, thanks to the Stuarts, the opportunity to talk about the Battenbergs and then—for that was the point he wanted to make—about their cousin Noronsoff whom, he announced in an affected voice, had been received often in his house (finally we were at the heart of the matter). With a quaver in his voice he evoked their magnificent villa 'Le Belvédère' in Villefranche-sur-Mer (where, of course, he was 'always welcome'), under the admiring nods of an Italian ready-to-wear clothes manufacturer's wife, whose nipples, turned down towards the ground, appeared, like two brown verucas through her clinging tight white nylon brassiere. Then, to show that snobbism was not the real aim of this digression, he talked movingly about the beauty of the youngest Noronsoff, a young man he called familiarly by his first name 'Ivan', displaying now his admitted vice (homosexuality) in order to better hide the less noble sin that followed: slander, to which he finally gave in, by announcing the imminent downfall of the family and the closure of their Vermouth factory.

Finally at ease, Claude could attack his tepid meal the girl sitting next to him had kindly covered with a napkin.

These dinners dragged on and on. Only Ben Chemoul, who for the occasion covered his ever-present underpants with an Indonesian batik draped like a sari, burned with a certain energy. Once his hunger was satisfied, Claude became bored, as one did at his age. In fact he was convinced he had better things to do than to be sitting there, listening. He would have preferred, for example, to be in Cannes with his sister, for he still thought that 'real life' was elsewhere. That sulk prevented him from enjoying the food, which he chewed without paying much attention.

At the table, the conversation was about the trivialities which usually preoccupy rich people, subjects whose variety or disparity were all too apparent. The pleasures promised by money and the obstacles the poor placed in the way represented the common ground for all those exchanges. Dissatisfaction and disgust were expressed and repeated with a violence proportional to the importance of the guest (a big German-speaking Swiss excelled in that range). Instead of being satisfied to consider, like Claude, that sensual delight was elsewhere (in Cannes, for example), these adults bore a grudge against those they held responsible for their boredom: badly-trained servants, striking airport staff, lazy builders, dishonest speedboat renters, invasive campers or sick prostitutes. Resentment took different forms, from irony to nihilism. "We'll never go back to the Voile Rouge," cried an ex of Sacha Distel with tears in her voice, disappointed with the welcome given by the beach boys.

The worst insults were reserved for those, male or female, whose charms had been designated for shared appetites: like a young actress, praised to the skies then trampled underfoot, first by those with whom she had cashed in her intimacy, and then, mimetically by the others. Women especially contributed their venom: a nineteen-year-old beauty who had offered her marvellous youth to 'old friends' suddenly became a 'fat cow', a 'dustbin', a 'rotten vagina'. Ben Chemoul salivated in front of these mean words. He poked fun at his friends, arguing that 'Charlotte' or 'Valérie' were still quite 'fresh', seeing little girls, whom he had known as virgins, dragged into the mud and covered with turds by shopkeepers with saggy breasts and photographers with manicured fingers. Their excesses made Claude feel uncomfortable; they reminded him of the insalubriousness of his own and his sister's situation. At sixteen, he still imagined, like the other children, that meeting someone was going to shield him from the precariousness of his life. He

thought that an influential friend, an apartment of three hundred square metres in La Muette and an English car were waiting for him in the dowry of a kind of female Ben Chemoul who
resembled superlative actresses like Françoise Fabian or Anouk
Aimée. A guardian angel who was going to offer him board
and lodging, tenderness too, and allow him to devote his time
to the art of poetry.

Once, on an old road that led to La Belle-Isnarde, he had
caught sight of a woman with a towelling turban in a yellow
Dino Ferrari who had seemed to correspond to his aspirations,
but she hadn't looked at him. Ben Chemoul, in whom he had
confided, had made fun of him, telling him he was too young
for forty-year-old women, and that he'd better aim at the 'older
generation' who liked 'babies'. The Baron, a depraved German, had raised the stakes, proposing to introduce him to a
septagenerian who could give him a thousand francs to caress
his legs. Claude didn't like these blatant schemes for, because
of his youth, he lacked the necessary lightness to endure them.
He wanted a serious friend, whom he liked to imagine as an
antiquarian or fashion designer.

"Basically, you want a poof, but in a woman's body," little
Christophe had told him, sensibly.

Basically, that was it.

When little Sylvie's warm thigh came to rest against his at the
end of the dinner, while she was joking with an old faded nightclub owner with the hand of a butcher, he frowned, convinced
that he would have had more chance to find his benefactress
in Cannes. And later in the night, when he woke up hearing a
shutter banging or little Sylvie screaming beneath the assaults
of someone or other, he went down into the garden to dream.
A protective moon appeared between the spikes of the aga-
ves. Being by nature a man, he was not tied down by the same
drudgeries as his friends who were girls and, not having to give
too much of himself, he considered his present life as a long
holiday without any tomorrow other than the eternal return of
the sun, the morning brioche and useless conversation.

At the time, all adult preoccupations seemed to him as deprived of meaning as those conversations at table evoked earlier, or even, when he stopped being attentive to that background noise, like the sound of the Italian commercial radio station he used to listen to on those nights, all by himself, on the radio in Ben Chemoul's car. The main motives which underlay society: profit, lust, power, were as mysterious as the language of the shrill radio announcers who intervened between the songs of Umberto Tozzi or Gigliola Cinquetti. Failure to adjust—which one thinks of as invalidating—had not been corrected as yet by the obligations of adult life. As with every infirmity, it left room for the abnormal development of a different kind of sensibility. A richness of the soul which expressed itself when he slammed the heavy door of the Rolls Royce and let himself be guided by the song of some nocturnal bird. He didn't hear the language of the birds like St Francis of Assisi, the emptiness left in that pure heart by the lack of interest in what excited the majority of people, was naturally filled with God's call. The song coming from the dark of the night, tinged with the blue of the promise of dawn, recalled the simplicity of the principle of adoration.

"And where am I supposed to put my Archbishop?"

The question was posed to Ben Chemoul, one sparkling morning of the 14th July, by a young man of Oriental type wearing mirrored sunglasses and a pair of dirty trousers, but endowed with the low and melodious voice of a barrister at the height of his power.

"I can't put him in little Eva's bedroom. Two cows expecting the bull, that won't work."

Having said that the young man spread his naked and filthy feet, whose nails were as sharp as claws, on the table right next to Ben Chemoul's bowl of tea, a Breton bowl with the name 'Maurice' painted on it, that Sophie had offered him at the time of their romance.

"I hope you have a badminton court at least."

When one caught sight for the first time of a person who was going to be part of one's life for several years, it was rare that one didn't feel a kind of disagreeable premonition. On the day of their meeting, the Oriental failed to please Claude, and even frightened him slightly. Our hero was, however, used to 'creeps' as Niki used to say, but in the same category the suspicious character Eva had met at the funfair in La Foux, and with whom she had become infatuated to the point of bringing him back to sleep at the farm, could easily claim the prize. It was seriously stretching the rules of the small community. Ben Chemoul who was suspicious of the police, hated to have strangers imposed on him, though he thoroughly enjoyed the so-called 'Ali'. He could sniff something, something which was not his slightly strong body-odour, which reminded him of an adult goat; no, a perfume of snobbery and luxury. That boy had a true 'address book', he could 'feel it'. Besides, Ali reminded him of somebody, a Getty or a Rockefeller to whom he had attended in a rest home: as filthy, as unkempt, as restless. In a word, 'a crazy loaded with cash.' Ben Chemoul, who lived off his acquaintances and whose main talent, except for cooking, was to put people in contact with other people and to draw benefits from those meetings, congratulated himself on never making a mistake when he had such intuitions. Which was just as well for the mythomaniacs circulating in that part of the Var coast were numerous. And Eva was not just anybody, she was related through her mother to the rich financiers, the Goldsmiths. You could drop her in the shabbiest of places and she would immediately spot the well-off drug addict among the losers.

"Where's the phone? I need to call the Opels."

Pulling Claude by the chin, as if he were a child:

"Not the car dealer, little one, the head office!"

Ben Chemoul was all ears, the von Opel family villa was one of the most beautiful on the coast, and some of its descendants were known for having loose morals.

"The old queen gets up early. I'm going to tell him to get it together. We're going to have some fun. He's one of a kind and, on top of that, he speaks Latin. Not bad, he could help you with your homework, little boy!"

Driving an Austin Mini Moke, the Archbishop arrived with his Vuitton trunks. He was an old man of Jamaican origin, who, in the past, had been the highest Anglican prelate in Santo Domingo. Close friend of the Archbishop of C, he would call attention to himself when, the following year, he fell into the Thames, dead-drunk, during the Queen's Jubilee. At eighty-two, he had two avowed passions: badminton and Latin poetry, as well as a number of shameful passions for which Ali played Petronius. Ben Chemoul immediately relished their company, and in his turn the Archbishop appreciated the simple and rustic atmosphere of the country house transformed into a children's home. The small community was enriched with the presence of the kind old man, whose conversation and mind were the delight of the famous diners dear to the child-psychiatrist. Only Eva, who was very jealous, never called Monsignor Johnson by any name other than 'the old queen' and remained insensitive to his charm. Sophie, whom it was hard to befriend, fell for both of them and even offered them both a Breton bowl: 'Robert' for the Archbishop , and 'Alain' for Ali, as his name was not included in the series. The only serious nuisance caused by the new friends of the house came from the sexual preferences of the prelate. Virtually every night, Ali was charged with bringing back one or two men of North African or gypsy origin, whom he picked up in town or at the funfair. This created an unpleasant feeling of insecurity among the little gang. Especially after Ben Chemoul's Porsche-design sunglasses had been stolen, as well as a pair of his underpants drying on the line.

Claude reserved judgement until circumstances encouraged a closeness. As often happens, bad motives produced fortunate consequences. We are forced once again to bring to light the changeable disposition of our hero. From a very young age, he had been able to adapt to people and circumstances with a suppleness that general opinion condemned under the name of opportunism. So it was firstly the Archbishop's mini-jeep which attracted the young man to that interesting but immoral companion. Slightly tired of the joys of the moped, Claude saw in this new means of transport a promise of emancipation.

Besides, Ali insisted that Claude study Latin several hours a day. That former pupil of the Ecole Normale Supérieure, who had abandoned the garden of Greek and Roman antiquities for the more arid zones of Orphean vice, took an interest in the young man's fate. With one of those traits of generosity which distinguish a lost soul from a vulgar debauchee, he tried to preserve in the other what he was wasting in himself. In the ruins of his spirit survived some intact sections of that great edifice. Overcoming the destructive effects of drugs and alcohol, he suddenly managed, as under the effect of an inspiration, to reproduce, from memory, a few pages from Virgil, preserving for a moment, in the manner of his Arab ancestors, a tradition neglected by the western world. From that corpus, they could begin work. Claude, discouraged by the Latin he had learnt in school, saw for the first time in those happy moments regions whose familiarity surprised him. Those shadows spoke to him in a difficult language but one that he understood better than that of Ben Chemoul's friends, and the effort he had to put in to associate with them definitely counted for something in his pleasure. Certainly the Archbishop's memory took the place of the traditional dictionary, which erects the screen of a dark forest where the unknown word must be sought often under a different form, like an elusive demon whose hold can only be grasped by the traditional incantations of morphology and the complicated processes of syntax. And as the Archbishop's vocabulary was vast, Ali's poetic instinct, based on the solidity of past work studying 'school Latin', helped Claude to access the difficulties, thus the multiple subtleties, the countless echoes which, beyond the simple beauty of the sound, give to the classic poems their true existence, comparable only to what the man able to perceive in the inland sea of the Mediterranean suddenly lit by one of those translucent flashes, those glories the sun opened for the one who bends forward to look, sees:

the marvellous totality of the sea beds where the colourful fish, but also the drowned men with algae for hair, the wrecks and treasures, the deities with shells for eyes, the star fish randomly scattered around cauldrons and swallowed cities, sleep but respond silently in the manner of things. It was as if the simplicity of day-to-day visions had suddenly regained their primordial place, which delights us thanks to one or other verses from the poems of Virgil. A simplicity which has been lost without any reason or advantage to us because of the worries that so-called reality imposes on our consciousness.

It sufficed for Ali to interrupt his word by word translation to recite from memory several verses in one go—a little like a conductor during an orchestra rehearsal, whom having made each group of instruments practice their parts resumes for a moment that magic undertaking and makes us feel for a few bars through his interpretation Beethoven's profound intentions better then if we had listened to the entire symphony—for these verses reanimated with their breath some element of the world, the morning landscape, a grove of trees seen in silhouette against the sea, a soft rock warmed by the sun, and nature vibrating in contact with man, like those fairy-tale princesses for whom one single kiss was enough to render them sensitive to their lovers' embrace. Every person that heard his voice, in a moment of inactivity, forgot the false charms that humanity finds in its day-to-day preoccupations and was amazed by the grace of the old poem which illuminated the possibility of a life that one could finally love.

Little Sophie enjoyed, thanks to this, one of the rare respites in her short and violent existence. When Claude looked up from the columns of letters whose code he had just laboriously deciphered, he could see her on a small openwork wall of concave tiles, her chin resting on her knees, her face washed of all make-up, her hair loose and in waves set by the sea-salt, touching her naked feet, and behind her, but without her being detached from her background, the landscape, the creased silver of the sea, the rocky arch of a promontory awash with foam, the oblique pines, the vines, the prickly-pear trees, all living substances bound by the light, wind, and scents. The curls of her mortal hair answered to the sea's folds, the white foam, the stirring of thorns, the fast pace of the small clouds floating above; but the wind and the light were only a repeat in a major key, a second harmony, an added glaze, facing the muted, subterranean chord which rose from the ensemble. Never would the little girl belong to the world more than in those moments when she smelt the scent of warm bread on her knees and the caress of the wind on her back, while listening to Ali's voice, and never would the world be more propitious for her until the future day when, destroyed by her failed ordeal, her body would rest in Roman soil. We are not entirely aware of these things. But if our conscience doesn't inform us immediately, an obscure feeling of harmony, a slackening of the nerves, a sudden felicity should warn us that we are living, as they say, 'the most beautiful moments of our life.'

When the man of art accomplishes a masterpiece, he finds himself in the situation of a manual worker who forges new tools, not knowing what they're going to be used for, a mysterious operation is accomplished and doesn't cease being active for a long time after the man, and sometimes even his masterpiece, have disappeared. This renewal is not reduced to the forms used, whose number is finite, to the assemblage techniques, whose perfection is nothing but progress and thus repetition, to the materials least of all, whose different nature and molecules show from which civilization they date, to the preconceived idea, to the plan, whose putting into practice always disappoints or is diverted, but to life itself, which appears unexpectedly. Exhilarating inspiration, carries far away the miseries one is wrong to be surprised by—that overwhelm men of genius without restraining them entirely—blowing without ceasing on the work those men have accomplished even if their voice been silenced or the effigies they sculpted are buried again in a matrix of coral or alluvium, and even if the work needed to extract them is beyond the capability of one but necessitates the intervention of several. That same life, the conjugated efforts of Ali, the Archbishop, Claude—their non-scholarly pupil and the wind, were sufficient to enable the words to just reach the little girl's temporal white shell, the conch, apparently lifeless, opening onto a soul secretly enslaved by emotion, and above all able, if the work of nature hadn't been broken by suicide, to transmit, thanks to her maternal language, a tiny breath of the old and shy poet to a child who perhaps, in her turn would have accomplished something. If that young girl hadn't been pushed into the emptiness by the false and melancholic impressions that had been imprinted on her sensibility by a disorderly education, psychology, drugs, and all the contemporary naiveties, those beautiful moments would have been less sterile. For—and it was the same for Claude, Ali, even more for the Archbishop—the fleeting emotions aroused by those readings were never enough to shatter the order of the day that lazy despair, perverse conformism and the solid chains of debauchery preserved from all improvement. A pessimism Ben Chemoul summed up quite well each time he saw the four of them on the terrace:

"Read poems to Sophie? May as well piss in a violin."

The irritation caused by those 'little poetry parties'—and above all, the prolonged absence of Marina—made Ben Chemoul's manners towards Claude worsen, to such a degree that his use of the Rolls was withdrawn. A privilege only the inner circle was permitted. The suppression of that privilege foretold other setbacks. He had to give up his bedroom to Pauline and Veronique, whom the master liked to have not too far away, and took shelter in a room without a window. As he was by nature helpful, they made no bones about treating him badly. Soon, nobody talked to him except to ask him to accomplish those little chores life in a community multiplies, distributing responsibilities to such a point that nobody does anything. And they used the most insolent tone. Washing up, loading the washing machine, sweeping, toilet-cleaning, slowly became Claude's exclusive activities. Ben Chemoul, with that lack of thoughtfulness and respect for the people whom fate had put in his hands—shortcomings shared with most pimps—became less and less courteous with his old guest now fallen into disfavour. It goes without saying that the other members of the community were drawn to imitating him. Luckily for Claude, the loyalty of one girl corrected the effects of the general malignancy. Sophie, far from abandoning him—as the fickle Sylvie had done, who now called her old best friend 'Nestor', in reference to Captain Haddock's famous servant—made every effort to protect him. Detesting unanimity, she had found in this cause the opportunity to consolidate her resentment for Ben Chemoul ('a shit') and the others whom she called 'bidet scrapings'. Claude, who avoided conflicts and would almost have accepted his new status as galley-slave—childhood readings like Cinderella, had surely prepared him for that kind of humiliation—was pushed by little Sophie, in spite of himself, to rebellion, which cost him. Timid natures, whose weaknesses prompt them to the most humiliating concessions, are sometimes driven by greater weakness to acts of revolt. Fear of Sophie, whose favours he had enjoyed in the past, took over from the duty of submission he felt he owed his host. However he refused to poison the 'old guy' with rat poison, as the young girl had suggested. After a few outbursts, the doctor, who now watched Claude with the eyes of Saturn for his sons, decided to be rid of him, and straight away attributed that insolence, unexpected from such a wet rag, to the noxious influence of the two 'fags' whom he hadn't turned to immediate advantage, except for being relieved of a few personal effects and six crates of Bordeaux wine. As for little Sophie, she would complete the foursome for, as far as he was concerned, 'he'd had enough'.

So, on a hot afternoon in July, one could see driving past,

along the dusty track known as La Bastide Blanche, an Austin Mini Moke with its retinue aboard: an Archbishop at the wheel whose forehead was protected by a purple handkerchief; an Arab footman half-naked, softly singing a Donna Summer song; an alcoholic young girl dressed in a pair of silver Fiorucci jeans and a T-shirt advertising the latest Walt Disney film, *The Rescuers*, and Claude Boudin, buttoned up tight in his blazer with the Stanislas school badge, proclaiming the Bayard motto: *'French without Fear, Christians without Reproach'*. Secured on the roof-rack were two Vuitton trunks containing, as well as the prelate's necessaries, a few bottles of Château Margaux borrowed from Ben Chemoul, a pair of Porsche-design sunglasses and the notorious Eminence underpants, extra-large, which served from then on as a cloth to polish the clerical boots.

As soon as they reached Ramatuelle, the little company started to argue. Heat had dissipated the effects of the alcohol and the mood suffered as a result. Which direction to take was at the origin of the first argument. The Archbishop wanted to join some friends who had a hotel in Villefranche, Ali and Sophie would rather have headed for the nearest bar. As for Claude, he was day-dreaming about going to Cannes, as any attentive reader would have guessed by now. Those arguments stopped miraculously when Sophie left the flock after becoming infatuated with an itinerant melon-seller whom the Archbishop had already had his eye on for some days.

IN THE DISTANCE, about an hour's walk from the Croisette in the suburbs of Cannes, one would find in 1976 a modest neighbourhood that few holiday-makers knew about. Or perhaps they would come across it in their car, and for three reasons only: either they were lost while trying to reach the motorway; or they wanted to buy carpets at factory prices; or in the hope of sexual intercourse with an immigrant worker. There were a few pensioners living there, in little rented villas with one or two floors, but it was rather rare for those less fortunate people to receive visits, except from burglars. Besides, those old men and women didn't make much effort for the tourists and one could even meet some who were untidy and slovenly looking. Their neighbourhood was not on the town map distributed by the tourist office. Only the little posters appealing for votes for the candidates at the local elections reminded people that Cannes extended that far.

A Casino hyper-market had opened there in 1972, before the crisis, as an outpost for real-estate plans with no future. Since then, a clientele, made up mostly of old people, sat forever in the cafeteria gloomily contemplating their feet, or their empty cups. It looked like the television room of an old people's home. The commercial director, a middle-aged homosexual who would gladly have 'thrown all those derelicts into a gas chamber', sat lanquishing in the air-conditioning. He was planning to set up a new 'sleep zone', intent on replacing, next winter, the cafeteria whose turnover was laughable. He was hoping the customers of the new bed shop wouldn't have to be recruited from that dozing assembly.

When the manager lifted his eyes from his leaflets, he saw the two 'little punks'—as he called those new pests who had 'landed' a few days earlier—had taken up their usual place.

It wouldn't take long for them to fall asleep face down on the table, but for the moment, they seemed livelier than usual and messed about with a plate of dessert they must have 'lifted from the self-service'. The director had the uncomfortable feeling that they were having fun mimicking fellatio by using a banana Melba as their demonstration tool. How old could they be? Fifteen? Perhaps less. From afar, with all their make-up, they resembled the very young actresses in the musical *Bugsy Malone*. But from close up, it was a very different matter: a look, bags under the eyes, and a stench … It was actually much more *Taxi Driver*. Even then, the actress Jodie Foster was far from looking as 'lost' as these two. The worst bit was that they were rude with everybody, staring insolently at the rare 'normal' customers, laughing and making loud comments. Or they just flopped and slept like tramps. One could at least have hoped that they would make the old parasites go away, but they seemed to take a particular pleasure in frightening young mothers, teenagers, couples, the few people who 'brought any business' to the place. And they were not alone, they dragged behind them a bunch of losers who were scary, all of them crowded on the *piazza*, making access to the parking difficult when they didn't just burst into the cafeteria refusing to consume anything and taking over the toilet facilities for their exclusive use.

On that day it was already clear that things were going to get out of hand. The smarter of the two young girls had just spat a mouthful of whipped cream on the floor, after having licked her banana Melba in a very explicit manner. The director decided to confront them once more and to forbid them entry to the cafeteria in future.

Marina hadn't counted the exact time that had elapsed since they had fled from the brown apartment. A week, perhaps. One morning, seizing the opportunity—Leila had gone down to throw out the rubbish that littered the living room—they had run away. One certainty at least: nothing must remind them of the existence of that place in their future life. Nobody was ever

going to know. They had to forget. It was easy to act as if something or somebody had never existed, one just had to decide
it, and keep to it. Of course, for the moment, there were the
scars, the small fleshy dykes that had grown on their arms, their
legs, their bellies, some raised and some hollowed. The oldest
had finally closed, in spite of the sugar. They were as thick as
lips. The most recent, those which itched under the scabs were
irritated and didn't stop stinging, one of them, in the shape of
a triangle, was more of a bother because it prevented Marina
from closing her thighs, she would have liked to close her thighs
from time to time. And to have a wash. But that was impossible,
it stung too much. Luckily she still had some sleeping medicine,
some Nembutal and Bacardi rum from the hotel. And if one
wanted to see things in an optimistic light: they were not dead.
Contrary to the threats of the 'SS'. Zaza was the worst off for
it, she had become slightly deaf, and her right eye watered all
the time. It was probably because of the bite. Luckily they had
been able to take the punk sunglasses offered by Mr Piss-Three-
Drops, and some of their stuff, their make-up and money stolen from Leila's bag. Once out of there they had taken a bus, at
random, and had jumped off when they thought they had seen
a hotel Ben Chemoul had mentioned: the Carlton. But it was
not the right one. This one was too small, too rotten. It was not
called the Carlton but 'The Little Carlton'.

Looking at her friend 'messing around' with her dessert,
Marina nourished once more the melancolic thoughts that returned again and again, uncontrollable and unpredictable like
the physical pains that announce an illness. Most of the time
they were related to sexual matters.

To see these things done to another girl was a different matter.
On oneself it didn't count, one closed one's eyes, and it was as
if it was already done. But to another … Girls were like that,
they placed themselves more easily in the other girl's shoes than
in their own. The saddest thing was to have actually seen it. It
was also the proof that it had really taken place. The violence

that had been exercised on the little girl, and the way she submitted, closing her eyes—for it's easy to pretend to be okay with
a banana, but in reality, she was being forced. She opened her
mouth wide when her cheeks were squeezed, she let herself be
penetrated without a word, like a little dog. She closed her eyes,
she was undoubtedly trying not to smell the odour, she barely
wriggled, shifted slightly, probably because of the cramps, pins
and needles, for the position was uncomfortable. And all that
always lasted much longer than one thought. Marina had the
time to see her tiring under the assault, and to sense that she
was really low, really pitiable. She hoped on her behalf that it
was finished, but they started all over again. And even when
they had done their business, they found something with which
to debase her even further, they gave her crude orders, like:
"Go and wipe yourself". The most lousy thing was that they
could see nothing had changed afterwards. She had become
again like she was before, apparently anyway, still pretty, like
a stretched rubber she bounced back, she could be used again
as if nothing had happened, once, twice … And then suddenly
they had become angrier, they had decided to deal with both
of them, to mark the occasion, to make sure they would never
be the same. They were going to lose some of their self-esteem
and be diminished. That was the reason for the scars: to remind them. How could such things be permitted?

Moving towards the table with the two girls, the manager felt
apprehensive. He was scared to talk to them. He was annoyed;
they were watching him approach, so much so that he couldn't
retreat any longer, and he thought that really it was not his job
to be the police, he hadn't been employed for that. On top of
it, behind a window one can get all worked up, but when one
gets near enough to fight, it's like flirting: one feels the human
being, the waves, one is scared to hurt or be hurt. He was feeling
cold and his stomach hurt, though the cafeteria's air condition-
ing was not working as well as in his office. From close up they
looked pretty normal, especially the one not wearing sunglasses.

He even found her very pretty, she looked like Romy Schneider. To give himself courage, he spoke harshly to them. He was suddenly worked up for he had stepped in the whipped cream the young girl had spat out. That's when the pseudo-Romy Schneider started to insult him. And the other girl, rising slowly as if to obey her order, plunged something pointed into his throat.

The cafeteria had taken on a dark, slightly reddish colour. Marina could only hear some buzzing, and her own voice, which she didn't recognize, insulting somebody, probably the 'wideboy' in the suit who wanted to chase them out, and who now stepped back holding onto his neck. For a few days they had been drinking Bacardi with sleeping pills. They felt that their nerves were on edge. That kind of mess was predictable. When they heard the word 'Police', Marina immediately moved towards the door while Zaza, who had taken a large dose of Nembutal, stood up, calmly, amid the chaos. With her sunglasses, she resembled the little blind girl in the forties romance that Marina had seen at the cinema Duroc with her mum. A crowd had started to gather around her. One man, braver than the others, a young father whose wife was trying to restrain him, calling 'Jean-Marc', came closer. He raised his hand as to stroke her hair and then, with one blow, swept away her sunglasses. But the girl didn't react. Seeing that she didn't defend herself, they caught her and layed into her.

Leaving the *piazza*, Marina started to enjoy life again. She felt a weight had been lifted from her. With Zaza gone, no trace of the brown apartment remained. She only had to take her stuff from the hotel and she could start afresh. On top of that, the other 'sperm bag' as Leila used to call him, didn't even know her real name. Thinking about it, she realized that she hated that brat who had brought her bad luck right from the start. She was the 'poor girl', not her.

Live and let die. Marina liked that film title and, while doing her hair in front of a display cabinet, she decided that from now on, it would be her motto and she was going to change her identity.

From now on she would be called 'Stephanie.'

Ben Chemoul was right: a beautiful girl like her, so young, made-up and everything, took on average four minutes to meet a man on the Côte d'Azur. Stephanie met several. No one extraordinary, but sufficient. The last one, called Richard Choukroun (no relation with either Régine or Caroline), nicknamed 'El Macho' by his friends, owned a Porsche and a jewellery shop. He introduced her to some 'good' people who gave her a little hope for the future.

In a palace, silk and gold, in Ecbatane,
Beautiful devils, juvenile Satans,
To the sound of a mahometan music,
Stifle their five senses in the Seven Sins.
Now the most gorgeous of all these bad angels
Was sixteen beneath his crown of flowers …

Having reached that stage in his declaiming, Ivan Du Bonnet took Stephanie by the waist, flicked back his long chestnut-brown locks and laughed nervously. Stephanie, who thought that the poem spoke more to a boy than a girl, let her lover hug her. In spite of her young age, she had already noticed that some men preferred to be seen with girls while thinking about boys. A frame of mind little Laurent used to sum up with one of those phrases which were his speciality: which were his speciality: "If one's going to be bored anyway, might as well be with a girl."

Heir to a brand of Vermouth whose license dated from 1890, and above all, a Russian aristocrat through his mother, the tall Ivan liked to give decadent parties ('decadent' was his favourite word) at the family villa in Villefranche-sur-Mer. Some female visitors ended up there for quite a while. The good thing about bourgeois decadents—other than of course, their lifestyle—was that they left girls in peace. Their libido, still dormant—as Ben Chemoul would have said—didn't compel them to bring the

subject up all the time. That was refreshing. With Ivan, Stephanie spent her days quietly holding hands, watching television
or looking at the yachts in the bay through a telescope. Ivan was
proud to show that he recognized them all. Perhaps because his
family no longer had the means to afford one, the alcoholic
proletariat having abandoned Vermouth for aniseed aperitifs;
and perhaps because he was becoming like his father. Ivan was
capable of recognizing with one look through the telescope,
the old *Nabila*, a kind of small cargo-ship with a chimney and a
Panamanian flag that Adnan Kashoggi had sold to some Texan
oil baron, noticing that the helicopter on board had changed—
in one fell swoop pointing the telescope at the black sails of the
old *Zacca*, the schooner that had belonged to the actor Errol
Flynn, now restored by a Hollywood fashion designer. After
a while this telescope ballet made her slightly drunk, but that
didn't hurt anyone. Stephanie was laughing behind Ivan's back
with 'Polly', a horsey-faced blond girl who was 'having it off'
with Arnaud de C, another beanpole, hairy this one.

"His thing is old walking sticks. He has thousands hooked
to the wall in the living-room and you should hear him talking
about them, he gets sooo excited!"

One afternoon when Ivan was 'working' with his mother,
Stephanie, needing a change from the yachts, spied on the
Rolling Stones who were living in a villa at the bottom of the
corniche. She couldn't believe what she was seeing when she
caught sight, on the road, of her brother Claude in a jeep
accompanied by a blotchy old queen and someone ape-like
beside him.

If her brother ever found her and landed here with those two
fags, it would be the end. Stephanie-Marina nervously shifted
the axis of the telescope, hoping, quite childishly, that by no
longer seeing them she was making them disappear. She felt
as confused as the day she had come across an article in the
Var-Nice-Matin entitled *'Clockwork Orange in a Cafeteria in the Town
Centre'*.

'No pathos,' Ben Chemoul would have said, another character whose presence would have seemed odious to the young girl just now, especially since she was following his principles. Marina put the leather cap back on the telescope and went back into the house to contemplate once more the Yves Saint Laurent purse Ivan had offered her for her 'nineteenth' birthday (unaware that she was going to be fourteen in a month). She adhered to a ceremony she never performed without emotion and which relieved her momentarily from all worries. Taking the *shopping-bag* out of its hiding place (she didn't trust the chambermaid), after having caressed the thick and luxurious wrapping, she gently extracted the black box, which also bore the famous initials, and then sank silently onto the embossed satin of the bedspread. The young girl breathed a few times before raising the lid with a lateral movement of her two thumbs. That's when the real delights began: progressive unfolding of the silk paper, which scrunched under her fingers like the stiff brown paper used for storing Christmas cribs, but which she took great care not to crease, so that she could fold it back later. Then, marvel of marvels, the first apparition, a little bit of dark blue velvet, expensive-looking and promising depth, more then comfort, oblivion. Sliding the clasp of the plexiglass, removing the other silk tissue paper, the inner one, more precious, which no one would dare to crumple, her nose dived into the nocturnal velvet and breathed in the lovely smell.

A little while later, as she was gulping down the only thing she'd found in the kitchen, a container with a litre of ice cream, she thought once again about the American who had bitten Zaza, the one the other regulars of the brown apartment used to call 'The Cuban'. He called her 'my little fiancée' and wanted to take her to Brownsville in Texas. It was he who had cut a tri-angle of skin from the inside of her thighs. He was the one she couldn't forget. She especially remembered his voice, and something he had said to her:

"You'll come to a bad end."

TO CELEBRATE ALI'S sixtieth birthday with dignity, they had decided to have lunch at Chez Nénette, a transport cafe situated near the boulevard MacDonald. Kind of half-way between them, for Claude was now living at 333, rue de Belleville, in a former hotel belonging to Madame Hélène, a new acquaintance. Claude was having his breakfast at the Zodiaque, a café close to his place, as he did every morning around eleven when Ali called him on his mobile to announce that he was cancelling—he was on a diet. Thus they decided to meet at Ali's place, for Madame Hélène didn't want Claude to have visitors.

At Ali's, Claude met Dominique, Ali's disciple. Dominique was a youthful script-writer with the face of a young priest whom Ali had picked up at a charity shop. The two men had 'got together' for a few days until Dominique took Ali back to his place on the rue du Ruisseau. That afternoon, Ali having sacrificed himself to their usual sexual ritual had been mildly surprised when, going to the bathroom, he had found a Winnie-the-Pooh and a toy lorry in the corridor. That bad impression had been forgotten as soon as he started to sing a few bars of a Charles Aznavour song in the shower. Then a female voice had started screaming in the living room.

"What on earth are you doing here? With a faggot again!"

While Ali was getting dressed on the landing (which hadn't happened to him since 1983), Dominique had explained quickly that he was not a homosexual but a father. Since then, their relationship had evolved into one of father-son, and, as Dominique had momentarily stopped writing scripts to enjoy fully his minimal income from the dole, Ali used him to help tidy his junk, especially his cards, into Tupperware boxes they had salvaged from the street.

"You look wonderful, Ali. You are slim as a thread."

Claude knew how to make his friend happy.

"Not bad, hey, since I started to do coke again. Do you know whom I bumped into in the Louvre des Antiquaires, Mother Du Bonnet. Well, she paid me a compliment, sort of."

Ali imitated Ivan's mother:

"How handsome you are, Alban (she always thought I was called Alban). When you were my son's friend, you had a weird look, but now, I think you're gorgeous. It's incredible how Aids improves people's looks."

"She thinks you've got Aids?"

"Of course since she thinks I gave it to her son. You'd think she might suspect the places he visited. New York on top of that, and in the worst period. I could see in her eyes that she was mentally counting the T4 cells I had left."

"Losing weight is bollocks."

That objection, coming from the depth of the broom cupboard, left Ali perplexed.

"Can you tell us why, Dominique, if you don't mind?"

"Do you really believe you're going to be more successful, that people will say, when they see you: 'How slim is that old guy! I'll have him.' "

"You'd better pay attention to what you're doing, you're trampling on Fabrice Emaer's card."

To avoid losing face, Ali pulled a Mick Jagger pout in the mirror.

"When did Ivan die?"

"In '86, more or less at the time your sister vanished."

"Do you know I found loads of pictures of us in Villefranche in '76! The famous decadent party with the Archbishop dressed up as Carmen Miranda."

"Did you bring the photos with you?"

"No, I think the Salvation Army must have got rid of them."

"Is the Salvation Army kind to you these days?"

Claude pictured Madame Hélène, his new protectoress, nicknamed 'the Salvation Army', and his heart sank.

"Yes, absolutely. Y'know, I saw little Veronique the other day. The one in love with Vince Taylor."

"Dominique! Do you know if Vince Taylor is dead?"

"Yeah, I think in '89."

"Can you find his card? When did she sleep with Vince Taylor, your friend?"

"She didn't sleep. She never slept—with anyone. They held hands, that's all."

"By the way, was it in '76 that we went to Mont-de-Marsan?"

"Perhaps in '77. I don't know, I remember we took Ivan's mother's car. Marina was furious, she was afraid we were going to steal her inheritance. But Madame Du Bonnet trusted the Archbishop one-hundred-per-cent."

"And your parents, they didn't care about you and your sister vanishing like that all summer?"

"Yes, of course they did, but Marina was supposed to be unable to talk. She pretended to suffer from a temporary aphasia due to the electroshocks. As she was in treatment with Ben Chemoul, I was supposed to be taking care of her and giving them news. Remember, in the Landes, we pretended on the phone that you were the manager of a Club Mickey specializing in children with special needs, while she was taking drugs in the toilet of the petrol station."

"Shouldn't we buy some heroin? You know, it's much cheaper now. There's some downstairs for eighty euros a gram."

"Oh no, not in the summer, it makes me sweat."

"What did we do in Mont-de-Marsan?"

"Can't remember, except we missed the 'Dammed' concert."

An exasperated voice came out of the cupboard.

"Not the 'Dammed', the 'Damned'."

"Oi you, you weren't even born, so shut up. Are they dead, the Dammed?"

The cupboard kept quiet.

"By the way, I borrowed a best of Charles Aznavour from the library. Dominique, do you mind putting it on for us?"

While the first bars of *La Bohème* made the walls and ceilings of Mr Milosevic's shake, Claude looked desperately in his friend's fridge. Like the gushing arrangements of Charles Aznavour's song, the cat's meat had coloured with a bloody trace its sole neighbour on the shelf below: an old Taillefine yoghurt, 'prune flavoured', the least-loved in the pack of twelve that Ali must have devoured with the gluttony characteristic of people on a diet.

"I have some kiwis, if you want."

"No, thanks."

Closing that sepulchre, Claude saw a *Pariscope* lying on the floor whose cover was devoted to the film: *Life is beautiful*. That title suspended like a crown above Roberto Benigni's bald pate, depressed him for he thought that as far as he was concerned, the worst was still to come. His kind of alopecia didn't work well with his hair long, but as it was frizzy, it was even worse.

"Dominique has found Marina's card!!!"

"Let's see!"

On a piece of yellowed card, a brand new looking photo of Marina was stapled, which Claude had totally forgotten. It had been taken in a café. The girl was tanned, with the tip of her nose peeling, her hair stuck together by the sea-salt was thick, abundant with life, not like the dry mossy tuft that Claude refused to cut. Her teeth too were sound and her blue-green eyes had not yet taken on the dusty film which seemed to dull adults' eyes, a bit like the greasy glaze which makes Tupperware boxes turn grey. The eyes were even brighter because the picture had been printed on a Agfa colour paper with a dominant blue. It looked like the photo-shoot of Alain Delon and Romy Schneider that *Paris-Match* had made during the shooting of *The Swimming Pool*.

Claude read the last lines of Ali's card, almost surprised to find no new information. What had really happened?

In June '86, a certain B, who was sharing a apartment with Marina, had informed the police of the disappearance of her flat-mate. B, a hairdresser and dress-designer, who worked from home, was not known to the police and her testimony didn't arouse any suspicion. The thesis of Marina running away to avoid paying the rent had been put forward, and since then, nobody had heard from Marina, nor Stephanie, nor Anne Du Bonnet born Boudin, her only real name. Marina had married

Ivan in '79 with his family's blessing. They had preferred to avoid Ivan's other plan: a gay wedding in Holland to Ali.

At the bottom of the card, Ali had written in pencil, the address of her last known home:

Agua Verde Condo appt 969, 401 Ring gold Rd,
Brownsville, Tex 78520 USA

The plaster virgin which occupied a place of honour in one of the chapels of the Sainte-Marie-Médiatrice Church had seen many penitents in front of her altars, but this one was particularly pathetic. With his shapeless boots, his old blue jeans and bowling shirt on which the name 'Claude' was embroidered in baby blue, not to mention the rare mossy hair that he had tried to gather on the top of his head (from the Virgin Mary's viewpoint, on top of the altar, it was the only thing visible), he inspired pity—the only feeling, by the way, that the industrial workshop had succeeded in breathing into the insipid physiognomy of this representation of Our Lady of Fatima. The man was preparing to make his confession with the priest on duty that day. The only other member of the congregation was an old lady busy looking after the candles, who was wedged in a bench in the last row. She noticed that her neighbour-in-prayer was crying. What a shame, she thought, such a handsome man!

The reader, now used to our biased comments, has obviously guessed that, like Claude Boudin, we have something to confess. The crux of the story. The secret which pushed our hero to kneel in a confessional made of varnished pine, concerned of course the circumstances which surrounded or rather anticipated Marina's disappearance. The priest was Portuguese and Claude had difficulties telling him his story. Here are the facts, summarized:

In 1985, Claude went to visit his sister in California. Marina lived on the outskirts of Los Angeles, in Redondo Beach. A

French girl, a certain Niki, had come round to have her hair done. Claude and Niki had spent that first day together. One evening, Claude had accompanied N to a dealer's place. There they met Sara, a Mexican woman, who had boasted of being six feet tall, and also about organizing 'cheerleader competitions' with her associate, a guy wearing a cowboy hat. They hadn't stopped squabbling about Satan. The man with the stetson had taken Claude aside, and offered him money if he gave him Marina's address for—he pretended—one of his friends was in love with her. He just wanted her address, nothing more, so that he could send her some dried flowers. Under the influence of heroin, Claude was finally persuaded (more so for Niki had just discovered that she had left the money for the drugs in the taxi). They both decided not to say a word about the incident. Three months later, Claude had received a horrible letter from Marina, sent from Texas. He had destroyed it. In 1989, in Majorca, he had discovered in the magazine *Detective,* that the Mexican woman was a witch.

By hardening us, the betrayals diminish us, and if the person who, in the past, wanted to be called Marina is still alive somewhere—which is what the humanist reader surely wishes—let's wager that she has become, under a different name, an altogether different kind of person. If she had failed to wean herself off the opiates early enough, by following one of those programmes for drug-addicts that western states have set up almost everywhere, her ghostly existence must be drawing to a close on the outskirts of some urban centre. But let's not be cruel: let us imagine her clean, living today in Florida, Venezuela, London, Switzerland or in any of those places where money and, consequently, prostitutes are abundant. At forty-one, her career is far from finished, the price of her services could even be rising thanks to some perverse speciality. Or, having come off heroin young, she may have won the 'jackpot' in the form of some 'pig' she married before she reached thirty. The structure of her face, the rare colour of her eyes, the quality of her skin can still give her real satisfaction. The advance in skilful plastic surgery having done the rest, she passes for a very attractive thirty-five-year-old woman. She must still love the sun and perhaps she is stretched on a Mediterranean terrace at the very moment this is being written. Alas, if since 1976 the sun hasn't changed, nor the trees with their odouriferous essences which gave the atmosphere of the period its perfume—the more chemical scents of monoï or of bergamot mix, behind which the other scents rise as before, at the end of a certain length of exposure, varying according to the speed of sweating—the odour of warm bread as one's own flesh heated up by the warm stone with essences of sulphur—if everything is still there, nothing is the same, for the nervous centre where the information transported by our senses reforms to build the great poem of man and nature, that centre the idealists call the soul, that centre doesn't react any more, or rather it doesn't accomplish, like a diseased organ, the work which at sixteen it trifled with, causing at each moment marvels and treasures that no currency, even a strong one, can ever procure. In fact it would be enough for her to open her eyes, perhaps protected by the very same sunglasses launched in the Italian press six months earlier by the cold Medora and her fellow models, for the destruction accomplished to be revealed to our eyes. Something has changed. It's not the wrinkles at the corners of her eyes that are easily smoothed out with Botox, even less that discolouration at the edge of the cornea that gerontoxon, also called senile arch, that age, alcoholism or syphilis can cause in some subjects. No. Her healthy life protects her against these degradations. It concerns the disappearance of something else, a minute sparkle some people always lack, fragile and not long-lived, it nevertheless protects, as long as it shines, the person who guards it against the suffering of the spirit which it always denies. It can last one hundred years, or disappear in one day: it's called grace and it's no longer in her.

After his confession Claude returned to his 'night shelter' at

333, rue de Belleville. There he thought about his meeting the next day at the lawyers with Medora Du Bonnet, to settle his parents' inheritance. Finally, he hoped, he would be able to leave this hovel and settle in a little house in the countryside. Finally, to be alone with his books and the few objects he owned. He could picture himself like Des Esseintes, the hero of the novel he liked, buried in Tertullian's work while savouring a Swiss lentil soup. But first he had to sign some papers with his snobbish niece, by whom he was slightly impressed. He wanted to make a good impression. Later he would try a new regenerating shampoo with a 'miraculous volumizer'.

He tried to read the time of the meeting on the papers from the lawyer, but he had left his reading glasses at Ali's. The 'Salvation Army' would shout at him again for it was the third pair he had lost. Stressed by that prospect, he swallowed a handful of self-tanning pills, hoping to look superb the next morning.

This time he didn't screw up.

For his funeral, Madame Hélène, with Medora's agreement, pooh-poohed pomp and sumptuous expenses for the good taste of sobriety, consistent with their shared taste for economy. Cremation with a scattering of the ashes in the Thiais cemetery. Unfortunately Medora couldn't attend the ceremony, she had a photo shoot abroad. Abbé Billot delivered a moving tribute, even if his mental faculties, weakened by age, lead him to forget, several times, the name of the deceased whom he once called 'Alain', then 'Patrice' and even, in a moment of bewilderment, 'Isabelle'. Ali read a few verses that Claude liked:

We will walk thus, only leaving our shadow
On that barren land where the dead have passed;
We will speak of them at the time when all is dark,
When you are pleased to follow an erased way,
To dream, supported by uncertain branches,
Crying as Diane at the edge of her fountains,
Your love taciturn and always menaced.

After the cremation, Ali refused to have lunch at the nearby Mexican restaurant with the few people present. He was still on a diet. He took the metro with an old acquaintance, little Marc, who couldn't prevent himself, despite the circumstances, from posing the question that had been bothering him for some time. As they parted at the Gaîté stop, he enquired:

"Ali, do you think Claude had a big dick?"

The other didn't respond. He was engrossed by a young Romanian beggar whose eyes he found were the most beautiful in the world.

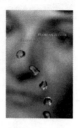

FLORIAN ZELLER

LOVERS OR SOMETHING LIKE IT

Translated from the French
by Sue Dyson

WHEN DISAFFECTED YOUNG PARISIAN Tristan meets
pretty, fragile Amelie he is thrown off guard by his feelings
for her. He had sworn to stay single forever, loving and
leaving a trail of heartbroken women in his wake. He hasn't
done anything to deserve falling in love: why him and why
Amelie? Is she really so special? Tristan is torn between
tenderness and desire, and as their relationship grows ever
more complex, he finds it impossible to avoid betrayal.
Lovers or something like it is an intelligent and sensitive portrayal
of the doubts and desires of a new generation, suffering
from the agony of indecision and too many choices to feel
true contentment.

FLORIAN ZELLER was born in 1979 and is a lecturer at
the University of Political Science in Paris. *Lovers or something like it* is his second novel and was published in France
to enormous critical acclaim. He received the Hachette
Foundation Literary Prize for his first novel, *Les Neiges Arti-
ficielles,* and the Prix Interallie for his third novel, *La Fascination du Pire,* to be published by Pushkin Press in 2006.

ISBN 1 901285 52 9 • 152 pp • £10.99/$16.95

PHILIPPE BEAUSSANT

RENDEZVOUS
IN VENICE

*Translated from the French
by Paul Buck and Catherine Petit*

PIERRE THOUGHT HE KNEW his Uncle Charles well. He had worked with him on a daily basis for fifteen years, assisting the austere art historian in his studies. Yet five years after Charles' death, Pierre finds a diary in which his uncle had written of a secret, heartbreaking love affair. When by chance Pierre meets Judith, the woman that his uncle so passionately loved, neither one mentions the affair, but the image that Pierre has of Charles is irrevocably transformed. Then Pierre meets Judith's daughter, Sarah, and soon finds that his own life will be changed forever. Beaussant's superbly crafted narrative effortlessly conveys the author's passion for art to the reader.

PHILIPPE BEAUSSANT is a novelist and musicologist. He has written several works of fiction besides *Rendezvous in Venice,* and is the author of numerous books on the history and art of the Baroque era. He was awarded the *Brive Prix de la Langue Francaise* in 2001 and the *Prix Littéraire du Prince Pierre de Monaco* in 2004.

ISBN 1 901285 55 3 • 128 pp • £10.99/$16.95

PUSHKIN PAPER

€ 11,50 Frax